DETECTIVE MOTHMAN

AND OTHER CURIOSITIES

CARI DUBIEL

DUSKBOUND BOOKS

CONTENTS

PREFACE

I've done a lot of book signings since I LOVED THE MOTHMAN came out in 2024. Since I have never been a supernatural writer, I've got a goofy spread of titles on my table: MOTHMAN, my nonfiction AUTHOR'S GUIDE TO LIBRARIES, and contemporary upmarket such as HOW TO REMEMBER. I always recommend that authors avoid writing in multiple genres because it can mess with their brand. But here I go ignoring my own advice again.

I've been bowled over by MOTHMAN's success. While I'm proud of my other books, I've never gotten so much attention for a title. And I'm so grateful to all those readers for their feedback and support.

As I was attending those signings, I found that I was telling readers that I was inspired by folklore. I started to realize that my lifelong connection with mythology is what has sparked my ideas for short stories. I was obsessed with Greek myth as a child, especially that of Andromeda. I couldn't fathom how a parent could tie their own kid up to a rock and leave her for a freaking sea monster. So with this volume, I decided to expand my scope. We're not just talking about cryptids here, people. We're going wide. And I think the next book in this series might go even wider.

Of course, we're still exploring some cryptid territory. There's the title story, of course, and "Guess Who's Coming to Dinner." Both of those were influenced by *Unsolved Mysteries* episodes on Netflix. I've learned about more cryptids spotted only ten minutes from my house in the Cuyahoga Valley National Park. I'm finally writing about the beloved Squonk, too.

If you would like to be surprised about the upcoming stories, I won't spoil them for you. But if you are curious and want to read the background of each before diving in, check out the Appendix at the back. You can learn about the creatures and the genesis of each story.

I'm so excited to share this book with all of you!

Cari
June 11, 2025

DETECTIVE MOTHMAN

Thank you, dear reader, for finding my message. You are my only hope in solving this dreadful mystery.

My story begins before the dawn of humanity. I myself have not lived this long, but my people have. We have haunted this earth for generations. I know we are frightening, intimidating, but we cannot reveal ourselves to you. You see, we have a gift: we can predict disaster. And we have no desire to reveal our gift to a society that exploits so many.

But we have tried to warn you. Some disasters are so devastating, so painful, that we have attempted to intervene. The Silver Bridge collapse in Point Pleasant, West Virginia, took 46 lives. I myself appeared to many humans in the effort to prevent those lives from being lost. I was young, though, and scared the townspeople. I hope to reach you now in a way you can understand. There is danger ahead.

A killer is on the loose in Chicago. Nothing I have done has made a difference—one person has already died. Her name was Alicia Stanley. If we cannot catch this murderer, at least thirty souls will lose their lives, and maybe more. This individual is a sociopath, someone who delights in taking the lives of others. But they are young in their career, just learning how to capture and kill their victims.

We still have the chance to save more women, but I need your help. You *have the tools to solve this case. You can walk around freely, investigate clues, report back to me with your investigation results. I will follow and protect you. We will not repeat the mistakes of the Silver Bridge.*

Thank you for taking on this significant responsibility. We will do this together.

❧

THE THREE OF them had been minding their own business, wandering aimlessly in Andersonville as they tended to do. Late spring, almost the end of school, unseasonably warm. Poppy was in her usual fairy-adjacent garb: green hair, flowing dress, combat boots. Gene plodded along beside them in an old Metallica T-shirt and worn black jeans. "He's in his Eeyore stage," Poppy had said once, and Nathan had replied, "He's always been in the Eeyore stage."

Poppy had her phone out with a compass app. She was into geocaching, the thing where people used coordinates to find little hidden packages all over the place. Nathan thought this was kind of childish, but he didn't want to yuck Poppy's yum. She'd been doing it since they were kids.

When she stopped, both Nathan and Gene almost bumped into her. The phone was pointing her to an alley. Nathan could smell the two trash cans sitting there.

"Ooooh," Poppy chirped. "There's something here!"

She squatted beside the trash cans and dug out a small black box with two red jewels embedded in its top, then drew out a piece of paper and handed it to Nathan. He scanned it, then crumpled the letter in his right fist. "It's a stupid prank," he told her.

"Hey!" Poppy hopped up, trying to grab it from his hand. "Don't throw that out."

"It's stupid," Nathan said, but his heart was racing.

God, he'd always been in love with her. Her tiny hummingbird energy, her curiosity, her kindness. She was the manic pixie dream girl embodied: the perfect girl who seemed vapid on the outside but was so deep on the inside. Nathan dreamed of the romance, the sweep of emotion he'd feel when he pulled her into his arms. They'd fit together perfectly, like a key and a lock.

Gene kicked the sidewalk. "Nathan's right. Let it go, Poppy."

She put her hands on her slim hips as Nathan aimed for the trash can. The letter flew above her head as he landed the shot.

Poppy bared her teeth. Her hair frizzed around her head, as if it was just as indignant as she was. She reached in, her feet rising as she leaned over and plucked the letter out of the trash. There was now a suspicious green fluid covering the letter's back corner.

Gene frowned. "Gross."

"Whoever this is, they need help." Poppy, who was quick to emote, raised her hands to her cheeks. Her eyes already shone with tears. "This is serious."

Gene leaned over her shoulder and skimmed the note, then let out a guffaw. "This is some shithead playing a joke. Premonitions of serial killers? Let it go, Poppy. You guys want to hit up Simon's?"

"I'm sick of going to some bar every night." Poppy unfolded the note and smoothed it out. "I'm bored. Let's shake this place up a little."

~

THEY ENDED up at Simon's anyway.

The bar was old but quirky. Its neon sign featured a blue fish holding a yellow martini glass and wearing a yellow hat. Inside, stained glass windows boasted images of the same fish. Nathan had never understood the symbolism. It was humid, the scent of beer hanging in the air, mixing with the smells of aged wood and walls.

Gene got a summer shandy. Poppy ordered an apple mocktail, and Nathan requested water.

Poppy extracted the letter from her pocket and placed it on the table. "Let's read this more closely."

"Is there green stuff in your pockets?" Gene asked.

Poppy made a face. "I don't know. Or care."

Gene rolled his eyes.

She peered at the text on the page. "*We have haunted this earth for generations... we can predict disaster.*"

Nathan balled his fists. His jagged nails scratched the inside of his palms. "Some kind of alien thing. Not human."

Gene groaned. "You gonna get in on this too, huh?"

Nathan shrugged.

"*The Silver Bridge.*" Poppy squinted, then tapped her chin. "I've heard of that before. Point Pleasant, West Virginia. Where have I heard of this?"

A server appeared with their drinks. Poppy whipped out her phone and started tapping while she sucked down her mocktail. Gene sneered again with that twisted lip.

"Mothman!" Poppy said triumphantly. "Mothman was at Point Pleasant." She consulted the letter. "He says he tried to warn them. It has to be him. Mothman wants us to solve a mystery."

"Dear God, Poppy." Gene slammed his beer on the table. "Nate, don't you agree? You said this was stupid before."

Nathan had said it. Had felt it. But as he watched her, that earnest look on her freckled face, he felt a spark of interest. Maybe this mission was important.

"I don't know," Nathan said. "Now that I think about it, it is kinda intriguing."

"Stupid. Y'all are gonna get kidnapped or killed or something." Gene threw back the rest of his beer. He patted Poppy on the head and scooted his chair away from her. It scraped on the floor as he got up and threw bills on the table. "I'm heading back. Don't stay out too late."

Poppy flipped a wave at Gene, but he was already out the door. She cleared her throat. "Okay. What else do we know? Alicia Stanley—the first victim's name. Should we be investigating her?"

A chill wiggled its way up Nathan's spine. This was going to end poorly.

"That sounds good," he said. "Let's go."

～

THE THREE OF them grew up together, bonded by being nerdy kids in a private school full of snobs. They were in college now, attending the University of Illinois. None of them had declared a major yet.

Poppy's parents sent her money sometimes. Nathan and Gene were on their own—Gene's parents had kicked him out, while Nathan's parents were dead. They were in their forties when he was born, and both suffered from diabetes and other medical issues that took them in their sixties. He'd inherited the house where he and Gene were living; Poppy was half an hour away, living in the dorm.

Inheriting the property had been like a sudden rainstorm: Nathan found out quickly that he had to care for the yard, pay for utilities and property tax, take out the trash—not to mention everything he was still dealing with through probate. His uncle had helped him, was still helping him, but most of the time Nathan felt like he was playing house. He'd had to grow up too quickly. No wonder he didn't know what he was doing with his life yet.

Nathan and Poppy found a bench lit by a streetlamp and huddled around Poppy's phone.

"It looks like she died just this morning." Poppy skimmed the news article that was the first search result. Then she put a hand over her mouth. "In the dorm. Like, my dorm."

"Shit," Nathan said in a breath. "Do you know her?"

Poppy shook her head. A green lock of curly hair fell into her face. "It's a big building. But oh my God. She was strangled."

"What else does the article say?" Nathan leaned in, feeling a twinge as he got so close to her that he could smell her hair. The warmth from her body radiated toward him.

"Not a whole lot. It's still breaking news." She lifted her head. "It does say that there were no signs of forced entry. The killer must have had access to the building."

Shit. "That means you aren't safe there, either."

"I'll be fine. I'm plucky, remember?"

"It doesn't mean you have superpowers." Nathan frowned. "I don't like you going back there alone. Especially if this guy is going to escalate quickly. Why don't you come to our place and sleep on the couch. At least for tonight. I'll grab an Uber."

She nodded. "Okay, I can see that. But in the morning we're going back to the dorm and sniffing around."

A warm, quick breeze blew across their faces. Poppy's hair lifted from her shoulders, and she grinned as the beat of wings sounded overhead. Nathan almost laughed at the silliness of it all, yet he also knew how serious their task was. He looked up to see the looming black shadow disappear into the sky.

SATURDAY MORNING, Nathan got up early and made breakfast. Gene crawled into the kitchen and started coffee while Poppy snored on the couch.

"You guys are ridiculous," Gene said. He slumped over the kitchen island while Nathan created a neat stack of pancakes on a plate. "Mothman. For God's sake."

"Well, what other plans do you have for today?" While the griddle sizzled, Nathan reached into the fridge for butter and syrup. "You might as well come with us."

Gene thumbed toward the TV with the XBOX hooked up. "Call of Duty calls."

They slathered their pancakes and gobbled them in no time. Both guys were fast eaters. Nathan, an only child, ate fast so he could go back to whatever he was doing. And Gene, with his big family, had to get his food before someone else did.

Nathan eyed the living room. Poppy was still not awake. One hand was slung across her face, and her hair fanned out behind her pillow in green corkscrews. He made sure to leave a couple pancakes for her, then pulled out his phone. Gene was breathing heavily as he scrolled on his own device.

With Alicia Stanley at the forefront of the news cycle, there were more articles. One this morning boasted a picture that Nathan recognized. She was in his geography seminar. That class was occupied by at least a hundred students, but Alicia was memorable. She looked a lot like Poppy: pink hair instead of green, round glasses, light purple lips. Not the typical sorority girl who died in these types of situations. Nathan's chest stung. He'd almost asked her out.

"Gene," Nathan said, snapping his fingers.

His friend looked up. "What?"

"Come with us."

"Why?" Gene's perma-scowl deepened.

"It's not the same without you." As much as Nathan hated to admit that, it was true. He could not concentrate with Poppy alone. And despite his demeanor, Gene was whip-smart. He might pick up on any clues the other two missed.

"I know you think it's stupid," Nathan continued, "but this girl died, man. And if we can prevent any more deaths…"

Gene stiffened, and Nathan flinched at his own words. Of course Gene didn't want to come with them. This was all too close to home.

But Gene recovered. "That's the thing." He pointed to the letter, which Poppy had thrown on the kitchen island where they sat. "Maybe whoever made that box was the killer. How else could they know the details?"

Nathan leaned against the counter. It all seemed so backwards. Either the whole thing was supernatural or the killer was leading them on a wild goose chase. Luring them into a trap, maybe.

Poppy plodded into the kitchen then, blinking sleep from her eyes. "Oh, thanks, babe," she said to Nathan as she beelined toward the plate he'd left her. The endearment made Nathan feel like a hammer was going through his head.

Gene yawned. "I have an essay to procrastinate on. You two go have fun."

Nathan didn't think tracking a killer sounded fun. But he couldn't handle the idea of more girls losing their lives. Gene left his syrupy plate, and Poppy took his spot at the island. Nathan couldn't help watching her as she ate, shoving pancakes into her mouth like they were the last things she'd ever eat. When she looked up, he turned away.

EVEN ON THEIR URBAN CAMPUS, there were pockets of green. The middle of the quad boasted well-manicured lawns and white birches with leaves hanging over the pathways between buildings. Sun filtered down through the leaves, dappling their path.

Nathan rarely visited the dorms—only for parties, and even then he wasn't much of a party guy. Poppy led the way, still in her dress from the night before. She'd thrown on a well-loved denim jacket that she'd left at Nathan's house once.

Their school was big enough that he didn't recognize anyone they passed. He felt anonymous, as if he weren't a student, just an interloper. Any one of these girls could be in one of his lectures, but they weren't the type he noticed. He preferred manic pixie dream girls.

Poppy scanned her card into the lobby. It smelled like any other dorm Nathan had been in: musty, old brick.

There was a girl behind the desk, a nothing girl, generic bleached blonde. Poppy went to swipe her card at the inside door, but the girl stopped her. "Only residents today," she said.

"Why?" Poppy looked puzzled. Nathan hung back, not wanting to break the rules.

The generic girl licked her lips. "Crime scene. Duh."

"Please." Poppy reached for Nathan's hand, and he nearly flinched. Her dry, warm palm was smooth against his clammy one. "I need my boyfriend to help move a TV. It won't take long."

Desk Girl's gaze landed on Nathan for a moment. "Can't you do that a different day?"

"I sold it on Marketplace." Poppy squeezed Nathan's hand, and all the nerves in his body lit with electricity. "The buyer expects it today."

"Oh my God, fine. But you better be out of there fast."

Poppy pointed finger guns at the girl. "You're the greatest, Kennedy. I owe you one."

Kennedy was still looking at Nathan. "Hey, you look familiar. Aren't you in my geography seminar?"

Nathan studied her face. She could have been any one of those basic girls sitting behind him, sipping on Frappuccinos and jawing about what someone was wearing yesterday in the quad. He wanted to be polite, though, so he nodded. "Yeah, I recognize you."

She smiled. "Well, it's nice to meet you."

He waved as Poppy tugged him through the door. As they stepped into the echoing corridor, she dropped his hand.

Nathan followed her to the creaking elevator and up to the third floor, where Alicia's room was. Not much to see—the door was criss-crossed with police tape. He guessed it was locked. Steps resounded along the hard floor, and an officer in uniform rounded a corner. Gun and everything. Nathan saw the frown before he clocked anything else about the guy.

"You're not supposed to be here." The cop pointed to Nathan. "Residents only."

"He's helping me move a TV," Poppy chirped. "Kennedy let me up. I sold it on Marketplace, so it needs to go today."

The cop narrowed his eyes. He was a gym bro, Nathan could tell. Buzz cut, square jaw. Behind that uniform was a set of muscles for days. Nathan hated that kind of guy. Talked a good game, but there was nothing behind the eyes. This was the kind of guy who dated girls like Kennedy.

"It won't take long." Poppy nodded down the hallway. "My room's just there."

"Alright," the cop said. "I'll wait. Leave the door open."

Poppy narrowed her eyes. "I have to change."

"Boyfriend can stay out here too then." The cop's hand moved to rest on his gun, and Nathan cringed.

"Why?" She lifted her chin. "It's not like he hasn't seen it before."

Nathan blushed a fiery red.

The cop groaned. "Fine. I don't care. Do what you need to do."

Poppy perked up. Nathan followed her into the room and shut the door.

She flopped on her bed and starfished on it—well, as far as she could extend her legs past the twin mattress. "Fuck that cop," Poppy said. "We should take a nap. He'll be waiting all day. Whatcha doing, Gem?"

He hadn't noticed that Poppy's roommate, Gemma, was lounging on the loft bed. Poppy and Gemma weren't attached at the hip. They had a decent relationship, but it was mostly superficial. Poppy had elbowed Nathan a few times, urging him to ask her out, but he couldn't do it. Dating Gemma while Poppy lived in the same room would be torture. She was nice enough, and he liked talking to her, but he didn't go for shy girls. He needed girls with flair and bounce. They kept him interested, kept him on his feet. Not that he'd had much of a relationship with anyone—not after his parents died—other than fooling around with a couple girls from the drama club in high school.

Nathan stood awkwardly above Poppy, where he could make eye contact with Gemma. She shrugged. "Same old. I wanted to hang out here before I go to Amy's."

Poppy aimed her voice in Gemma's direction. "You're spending the night off campus too, huh?"

"It's too freaky to be in here." Gemma shivered. She caught Nathan's eye, and he quickly looked away.

Poppy sat up. "I get that. Lana must have left too." Alicia's roommate, Nathan gathered.

"She's staying with her girlfriend on the fifth floor. That's where she was last night too. I don't think she'll ever go back to that room."

"Makes sense." Poppy glanced at the TV. "There's a cop outside waiting for us to move it."

Gemma frowned. Nathan felt like he was playing ceiling tennis as his gaze bounced between Gemma and Poppy.

"It was the only way I could get in," he said, clearing his throat.

"But why did you need to come in? You could have stayed outside."

He shifted from foot to foot, the wall looking quite interesting for a second.

Poppy got up and stood by him, craning her neck up to Gemma. "Seemed weird to make him wait downstairs. Well, I guess I'll tell the cop it was too heavy for us to move together. We'll have to come back with Gene."

"It's my TV, though," Gemma said.

"I know," Poppy said.

POPPY CHANGED while Nathan looked at the door. His cheeks hadn't stopped flaming. When he turned around, she was in a different floral dress with the same denim jacket.

She gave their excuse to the cop, who looked like he was straining not to roll his eyes. They ducked into the elevator, and Poppy pressed the button for floor five. "I'm hoping Lana is here," she said.

"Do you think she knows anything? If she wasn't even home when it happened?"

Poppy fixed him with a "really?" look as the musty elevator trundled upwards. "My dorm is not my home."

He supposed she was right. Unlike him and Gene, Poppy grew up with a picture-perfect childhood: parents who loved each other, sunny little sister. She was riding on a scholarship earned by her soaring grades. She had the flag line and her band friends. Poppy had a place to call home. Nathan had an empty house, and Gene was unmoored.

The elevator dinged and deposited them on the fifth floor. Poppy wandered the hall. No cops here–no crime scene. "I think her girl-friend's name is Rowan," Poppy whispered. "But it's a long shot."

Rowan's door was marked by a dry-erase board and a collage of magazine cut-out pictures. Poppy knocked, small at first but then louder. No answer.

She sighed. "Guess we should head back to your place. There's gotta be a different trail we can follow."

When they got to the first floor, Poppy avoided Kennedy's eyes. They clearly were not carrying the TV. They were out the doors and booking it toward the car when Poppy nearly bumped into a set of girls holding hands. Her eyes widened. "Lana? Rowan, oh my God!"

Seemed like a good time for Nathan to step back.

Lana's cheeks were tear-stained, and Nathan saw Poppy hesitate.

But eventually she took the breath that he knew would lead into word vomit. The jury was out as to whether that would produce answers.

"I know you probably have a million people asking questions," Poppy started. "But Nathan and I are working on this case and we need to find out as much as we can."

Nathan saw Lana's girlfriend squeeze her hand. He remembered the thirty seconds Poppy had held his.

Lana blinked. The warm breeze lifted the smell of turned earth off the grass.

"Working on the case?" Rowan prompted.

"Yeah. For... for Nathan's capstone project. He's shadowing the cops. This is the biggest case they've seen in years, and they wanted us to find as much information as we could. Especially since we go here." Never mind that Nathan was still a freshman.

Rowan narrowed her eyes. She was tall, with square shoulders, her body equipped to stare him down. "I don't recognize him."

Lana dropped her girlfriend's hand and finally spoke. "We don't owe them anything, babe. Let's just go back to your room."

"Wait!" Poppy called as they moved past. "They found fingerprints. I have to ask you, Lana. Who comes into your room when you're not there?"

"I'm not Alicia's keeper." Lana was small and hurt, like a baby bird, in contrast with Rowan's imposing frame. "She was quiet. Kept to herself. All I know is that the person had a key. No break-in. The cops slammed on Rowan's door last night at about three—they searched for me. Since I was the only other person with a key. But it scared the hell out of both of us."

Poppy nodded slowly. "That's helpful, though. Someone else must have had one."

"Yeah." Lana shrugged. "I won't know. We're getting out of this dorm entirely."

The women turned to walk away, and Poppy turned to Nathan. He felt like he'd faded into the background. Become part of the trees. "It's good information," Poppy said. "It was someone Alicia knew."

THEY WANDERED INTO THE CAFETERIA. It was more like a food court—students could swipe their meal cards for any type of takeout. Poppy put through an extra swipe for him, and he headed for the salad bar.

An icky feeling crawled down his back as he carried his plate to a table. It was only a little after one in the afternoon. They had no leads. They had no choice but to disappoint Mothman. Nathan felt stupid just saying the name in his head. It was that unreal.

Poppy placed her own salad in front of her and went to town. "We have to find out who Alicia knew well enough to give a key to," she said. "That'll narrow down our suspect list."

Leave it to Poppy to know which direction their investigation should take. Nathan took a few bites. His stomach hurt, and he heard it gurgle as he swallowed. Chickpeas and bean sprouts. They'd sounded good when he went through the buffet.

"Lana said Alicia was quiet," Nathan said. "I didn't think she'd have a lot of friends on social media."

Poppy whipped out her phone and started tapping. Her mouth was full, and she chewed around her words. "I shouldn't bother checking the usual spots then. Facebook and all that. I'll just do a Google."

He had nothing else to do but watch her as she wrinkled her nose and typed. Then she let out a surprised breath. "Alicia's on a microblog site," Poppy said. "Like what Twitter used to be, but not as many people."

Nathan nodded slowly. "So she posted on there?"

Poppy nodded back, her mouth still full. "She had friends on there. There aren't many, but we can Google them all. Blogs on this site aren't private."

"Why would she post on a site that isn't private?" Nathan finished the rest of his salad and pushed the plate away.

Poppy shrugged. "Maybe she didn't know. But the good news is that we can check out her profile."

He trailed Poppy out to the quad, where they found a bench. The lawn smelled like it had been mowed recently. Nathan had to clench his butt so as not to get too close to her on the small surface. Especially since he was leaning over her to see her phone. But she moved it close enough so that they could both see it, its lit screen shaded by the tree above. Her hip brushed against his, and he tried not to flinch.

She had to know. How could she not? He'd known her since they were ten. And she'd been brilliant even then, with that same impish smile. Her hair had been long and blonde and curly; she was a tiny princess.

She couldn't have the same feelings for him. She would have acted upon them by now. Though she was single now, Poppy had dated around since she was just fourteen. Girls and guys.

He relaxed. Who cared if his thigh touched hers. It didn't matter.

Poppy didn't notice. She was scrolling through Alicia Stanley's microblog feed, scrolling down, reversing, scrolling down again. "I thought maybe we could trace her movements."

"How so?" He didn't see anything on the site that indicated Alicia's position.

Poppy pointed to a picture she'd bypassed a few times. Alicia cheesed for the camera, holding a drink. "She's at a bar, right? Can we find out which one this is?"

"How can you tell? She might be in someone's basement." He didn't mean to play devil's advocate—he honestly couldn't tell where Alicia was.

"It's the lighting." Poppy pointed to Alicia's face. "See, there's a touch of green on the curve of her cheekbone, and there's the hint of a window on her other side. She's sitting next to a neon sign."

Nathan whistled. "Detective Poppy."

"Maybe I've found my calling." Poppy squinted. "The other thing–she had to be with someone. This isn't a selfie. If we can find the bar, someone there might know where she went afterward."

"Maybe." Nathan sat up straight and looked up through the branches of the tree they sat beneath. Clouds trailed through the blue sky. The day felt peaceful, like he should be sitting in the sun somewhere, letting rays play on his face. "If she was a regular there."

"Lana didn't say much about who Alicia hung out with. But maybe they didn't know each other that well. I still barely know Gemma even after living with her all year." Poppy peered at the bar picture, stared at the martini Alicia held. "What is that thing hanging from the glass rim?"

He blinked. The martini did look asymmetrical. He'd thought it was the angle, but there was some sort of object there: brown, almost like a stick, but bulbous on top.

She traced her finger into a shape around it. Then she sat up, tossed the phone into the grass, and shrieked. He startled and jumped up, and she did too, grabbing his shoulders and shaking him.

"I know where this is!" Poppy yelled. She picked up her phone and started twirling in a circle, her dress swirling around. "Let's go!"

Nathan texted Gene, and he begrudgingly agreed to go with them. *I'm kinda bored of Call of Duty anyway,* he wrote, and Nathan laughed. He'd never thought that day would come.

Gene met up with them outside the college, and they grabbed an Uber to the other side of town. The bar they were looking for was called Clever Girl. Outside of the whole "trying to solve a murder" thing, the place seemed cool. A T-Rex head hung down above the entrance, and green neon lights shone in the windows.

They scrambled onto high-top seats, and Poppy shivered. "This is where Alicia was sitting," she said.

Gene frowned. "You guys are still talking about this?"

Nathan elbowed Poppy. They hadn't told Gene this outing was part of their mission. She turned, eyes wide, and Nathan lifted his chin.

"I want one of those cute drinks," she said. "I bet they can make one virgin, huh?"

"Sure they could." Nathan motioned toward the bar. "Go find out. We'll wait for a server."

Almost as fast as they'd sat down, Poppy jumped back up and wove her way through the crowd. Her long braid and jean jacket went quickly out of view.

Gene turned to him, his expression sour. "There a reason you guys wanted to come here?"

"Something different." Nathan picked up the drink menu. "You want a beer?"

"Sure, yeah." Gene waved a hand. "I'm not feeling good about this whole thing."

Nathan winced. "Worried about her?"

"She didn't have to get involved." Gene fixed him with a hard stare. "Neither did you."

Nathan's face went hot.

"I get it, I get it, man," Gene said, but his eyes still glimmered with... what? Anger, annoyance, grief? All of that? "I know you're trying to protect her. Someone has to, I guess."

Nathan couldn't speak past the lump in his throat.

The server saved him, though. She was short, cute, with pigtailed hair a shade of red not found in nature. "Get you something?"

Nathan jumped in before Gene could say anything. "This guy'll have a Corona. I guess a Newcastle ale for me."

Pigtails nodded. "Be right back."

As the server disappeared into the crowd, Poppy came waltzing back. She held a martini with a plastic velociraptor clinging to the glass. "This is it!" she crowed as she bumped into the seat beside Gene. "This is the drink Alicia had."

"Did the bartender have anything to say?" Nathan asked mildly. Gene's leg started bouncing under the table.

Poppy shook her head. "There's too many people up there. We'll have to wait."

"You didn't tell me this was going to be a surveillance mission," Gene said.

She shrugged and sipped at the neon blue drink.

Pigtails came back and placed the beers in front of the guys. When she clocked Poppy, she smiled. "You came back."

Poppy lifted her drink. "Yeah, I made it back from the bar. I wasn't sure I would, honestly!"

The server blinked. "Weren't you here last night?"

Nathan questioned himself. No, they'd been in Andersonville, getting the note from Mothman. That seemed like so long ago.

Poppy snapped her fingers. "Oh, yes! I was here."

"With your other friend. You're a popular lady." Pigtails waved her hands between Nathan and Gene. "I thought you were dating the girl you were with?"

Poppy smirked and leaned on the table. "I'm not dating anyone."

THE BAR WAS EMPTYING OUT. Gene had left after a couple beers. He'd looked sad, Nathan thought. Frowning, gazing into his bottle. They'd pushed him too far, just because Nathan and Poppy wanted the trio to solve the mystery together. Nathan hadn't considered that Gene wouldn't want to unearth his old memories.

Nathan didn't have a sibling, so he couldn't have known how Gene felt. His parents had died, and he knew that grief keenly. But Nathan had cared for them both as they went downhill. He knew their deaths were coming. Gene's sister, though—she'd been young and popular. An unexpected tragedy.

Gene was very young when Kathleen died. For as long as Nathan had known him, Gene had been sisterless. His brothers were a pack, all gruff and solid. Gene's father was quiet, and his mother talked a blue streak, probably to erase the sorrow in her mind. Nathan had always known their family was broken. Something inside Gene had cracked.

"We shouldn't have brought him," Nathan said. He was into his third beer, but he'd spaced them out enough that he was nowhere near drunk. Not even tipsy.

"Who? Gene?" Poppy had ordered a few more of the velociraptor drinks, but they'd only given her one of the plastic toys. She played with it now, running her fingers over its head and the ridges that swept down its back.

"He's thinking about Kathleen. You know."

When they were little, Gene had wanted to play "funeral." Poppy had to play Kathleen. She would swan to the ground, and Nathan and Gene would pick her up and lay her out on a picnic table. Then they would all fake cry.

Poppy hummed. "I should have thought of that. I don't have any excuses."

"Me neither."

They were quiet for a while. Nathan could practically hear Poppy's mind whirring. He scrubbed a hand over his head. "We should probably go."

"No way." Poppy pointed. "Our new friend is on her way over."

Sure enough, Pigtails was approaching them, a wet towel in her hand. The server laid a hand on Poppy's shoulder. "Sorry, dear, but we're closing."

Nathan couldn't help it. He cleared his throat. The other woman's hand dropped from Poppy's shoulder.

"Listen," Poppy said, leaning in toward the server. "That wasn't me last night. It was a different girl. I know we look similar. I'm sorry I lied."

Pigtails grunted. "Why would you lie?"

Poppy grabbed her phone and pulled up the article about Alicia. She thrust the screen in Pigtails' face. The server moved back, squinting. "Holy hell," she said.

"Yeah. We're trying to find out what happened to her. You said she was with a girl?"

The server nodded. "Really pretty."

Nathan's ass hurt from sitting so long. He got out of the chair and stretched. Unless they could find out who Alicia was with, they were at a dead end.

"You probably don't have pictures of them or anything?" Poppy asked.

Pigtails twisted her lip. "That'd be creepy."

"Sometimes creepy is useful," Poppy said, then winced. "Never mind. No, no, it's not."

"There might be something on the camera." Pigtails pointed above the bar. There was a small circular lens Nathan never would have noticed. "I can't get the footage tonight. But if you want to come back tomorrow, I might be able to get my boss to pull it."

"That would be great," Nathan said around a yawn.

"We'll be back." Poppy winked at Pigtails. "I'm Poppy. Nice to meet you."

"Jen." Pigtails—Jen—smirked. "I'll see you soon."

Nathan couldn't sleep.

He'd been so tired when they got home–it was nearing three in the morning by the time they Ubered back. Poppy squeezed herself up next to him in the back seat and snored. He paid, of course, and dragged her back into the house and onto the couch. His bedroom was so quiet that he thought he'd conk out right away.

After tossing and turning too long, he got up and padded into the living room. Careful not to wake Poppy, he opened the sliding door out onto the porch.

The air was cool. Nathan sat on one of the Adirondack chairs and peered up at the sky. It was light, the sun already threatening to come up even though it would be another hour until that happened. He'd passed through the thick of night and now teetered on the edge of day.

His parents had bought these chairs when they built this house. He was little and the chairs were so big, red monstrosities. He'd sit all the way in the back and his feet wouldn't even dangle. Nathan thought of Gene: how much did he remember about his sister's death? Nathan barely knew anything about it. Shame nagged at him—why hadn't he been curious enough to find out? They'd been pulling Gene along for years, never letting him lead the way. Gene's tragedy was an afterthought, so back-of-mind that they hadn't even remembered Kathleen when they started this journey.

Nathan was getting irked at the creature who brought them the note that started all of this. He still had trouble believing that something called a Mothman existed.

He sat there and drifted off, fatigue finally overcoming him. He sat and tranced for a little bit, sort of sleeping, sort of awake. Like he was a night guard in charge of protecting the castle.

When he came to, his back sore and his brain muddled, he kicked to get up and found an envelope on the deck. He picked it up and tore it open.

Nathan,

I know you're going to feel guilty. Don't take this to heart. You have been doing well. You and Poppy will get down to the matter and save hundreds of lives. Unfortunately, we can't save them all. Gemma was the next to die—last night, while you were at the bar.

Gene said that he suspected me, but he couldn't be further from the truth. I was nowhere near the dorm last night. You'll see clickbait articles about where I've been spotted. I actually walked around last night, pretending I was in costume and posing with the ladies. There are pics of me everywhere.

Remember, Nathan, I predicted the collapse of the Silver Bridge, and there was nothing I could do to stop it. It is so unfortunate that Gemma had to die, but if it weren't for you, there would be countless others. Keep moving. I will check in with you tomorrow night.

The letter wasn't signed.

STILL DAZED, Nathan came inside to find Gene making coffee.

He handed Nathan a mug. "Late night."

"Yeah." Nathan felt like he could drop at any moment. He looked at Poppy, asleep and unaware, and dreaded telling her.

Gene rounded the bar to sit. "When are we going to talk about this?"

Nathan's gaze snapped to Gene's.

Gene motioned to Poppy. "I can't exactly play Three Amigos with you two right now."

Nathan took a sip from the mug. The coffee was bitter, strong. It heated him through his whole body, and sweat broke on his brow. He stood by the fridge as a vent blew lukewarm air down onto them. "I'm sorry," he said.

"Don't be." Gene took a long swallow. "I'll be fine. But Nathan–you're an idiot."

Nathan's head snapped up. The coffee churned in his stomach.

"She's never gonna love you, man."

They'd discussed this so many times. "I know," Nathan said.

"This is quite possibly the dumbest thing you've ever done." Gene snorted. "Mothman? What the fuck, Nathan."

"This isn't about Poppy." Nathan set his mug on the bar top. "If I can stop those girls dying…"

"You can't." Gene's voice softened a little. Nathan had thought Gene only had emotions when he was drunk. Something was crackling between them.

"Two girls are already dead," Nathan said.

"Lots of girls are already dead," Gene said.

Nathan had expected Poppy to wail, to pull her hair and gnash her teeth. Or whatever–cause a big drama. But she only stared at her phone, bent forward over the couch. He took a spot across from her on the recliner. It had been his dad's, and the leather still smelled of old times.

"What do you want to do?" he asked quietly.

Her long hair swung in front of her face, stringy and limp. She shook her head and massaged one temple.

"We can take it easy today," he offered.

"No." Her voice came out small. "That's my roommate. There on the screen. Like she wasn't a person just yesterday."

He understood. He knew the moment a person became a memory. "It doesn't mean you have to push yourself. We don't have to investigate."

Poppy raised her head. Her face was red and streaked by tears. "She said she wasn't even going to stay overnight. How did he get her?"

"I don't know, but you're safe. You can stay here as long as you need to. We have time."

She clenched her teeth. "We don't. What kind of killer can move that fast? Two girls in two days? Every day we wait could be another death."

"I can go out. You rest, and we'll regroup in a couple hours."

"No." She jumped up, her dirty dress swishing around her ankles. "I'm going. Let's go. It's all I can do."

Nathan wanted to tell her that sometimes there was nothing you could do. Instead, he said, "I'll drive you."

∽

THIS TIME, the authorities evacuated the dorm. According to college policy, law enforcement could only keep the students out until the crime scene had cleared; many of them had nowhere else to go.

It was a nice day. Sun blazing. Nathan's gaze traveled across the green, where most of the residents sat and waited to be let back in. Officers flanked the locked front door. College officials fended off a horde of reporters jockeying for comment.

Poppy plunked herself down next to Melissa, her RA, and Nathan sat gingerly beside them.

Melissa turned to Poppy, her gray eyes wide. She said everything without speaking. They hugged, both crying, as Nathan tried to embrace his awkwardness.

"What is happening?" Poppy wailed. Nathan wondered if this was when the gnashing of teeth would begin.

Melissa shook her head, her long braids bouncing. "This is insanity."

"Why would anyone..." Poppy began, but she lost steam.

"It seems random," Melissa said. "Like, they're targeting our dorm, but those two had nothing in common."

"There has to be a reason they're targeting our dorm though." Poppy chewed on a piece of her hair.

Nathan's exhausted mind churned. He was chewing on a thought, but he couldn't get it to manifest. His eyes were slipping closed even as he tried to listen to the women.

"There was even a security detail last night," Melissa said. "Even if someone had a key to Alicia's room, they couldn't possibly have a key to Gemma's room too... right?"

"My room," Poppy said.

"Someone like you would," Nathan said.

Both women turned to him. "What are you saying?" Melissa asked.

"I mean, not you. But someone like you. An RA or someone who worked in the building."

"So they've got access." Melissa picked at a blade of grass. "It makes sense. Easy targets."

Poppy blinked. New tears were welling in her eyes.

"There's another thing," Nathan said.

"They're both connected to me." Poppy dragged her hands over her red face. "Alicia looked like me. Gemma lived with me."

Melissa drew in a sharp breath. "Oh my God, Poppy, you can't stay here tonight."

"She's staying at my place," Nathan cut in.

Poppy set her jaw. "I need my things."

"I doubt they're even going to let you in, though." Melissa looked up, still twirling the grass between her fingers. "Your room is the crime scene. And it's safer for you to stay with Nathan. Especially if the person has access to all of us." She shivered. "I need to find someone to stay with me too."

"You're welcome at my place," Nathan offered. His heart picked up a little at the thought of a different woman in his house. Someone who didn't shred him every day as he stared at her on the couch.

Melissa waved a hand. "I'll figure it out. The residents need me. I just need a companion."

Poppy inched closer and bumped Melissa's hip with hers. "I'll stay with you."

It was Nathan's turn to clench his jaw.

The building was cleared an hour or so later. Campus catering set up on the lawn so residents could get something to eat. The girl behind the front desk was nowhere to be found, so Poppy marched immediately to her room, where the same officer from the day before stood again. Nathan cringed at the sight of the crime scene tape strung across their door. He felt Gemma's absence.

"You can't go in there." The man almost sounded bored.

"It's my room." She put her hands on her hips. "I need my things."

"Shoulda got them yesterday. I noticed that TV was still in there." The cop looked pointedly at Nathan.

"Just let me get my stuff and I'll be out of your hair. I'm staying down the hall with my RA."

That feeling pinched Nathan in the chest again.

The officer rolled his eyes and waved toward the door. "Let's go, then."

Nathan stood outside. A minute later, Poppy came back out, clutching a change of clothes, pajamas, and a green caddy full of toiletries. She sauntered down the hall, suddenly smug, and walked into Melissa's room. Nathan stood behind.

HE LEFT Poppy with Melissa and clomped down the rubber stairs with their yellow-painted walls. Bulletin boards lined each landing, covered with ads and announcements. Nathan stopped to scan over the headlines. *Spongebob Squarepants: The Musical! Auditions. Get your caffeine on at the Brew House. Candlelight Vigil for Alicia Stanley and Gemma Wright.*

Nathan's hands were squeezed into fists. Gene was right. After all they had been through, all he'd done for her, Poppy had blindsided him again. Nathan's only loyalty was to Mothman now. If Poppy was next on the list, he'd return to the dorm and fight for her. But only then. After all these years, he'd had enough.

He rounded the staircase corner, slipped into the dorm's computer lab, then signed in with his university credentials. Since that morning's conversation, he'd been curious about what happened to Gene's sister. It was a departure from the case at hand, but Nathan had been feeling guilty all day. With his eyes on Poppy, he'd ignored whatever his best friend was suffering.

The computers whirred, surrounding him with white noise in the dark room. He found a browser and typed. *Kathleen Burton.* And *Gene Burton,* for good measure. Nathan filtered the search to articles from their first-grade year.

University Student Dies in Tragic Fire, the headline read.

Nathan stilled as he scanned the story. Kathleen had gone to their college. Lived in this dorm. A candle tipped over, the article read. She was asleep. The fire hadn't spread far, but she died of smoke inhalation before anyone could find her.

His mind raced. He'd always thought Gene didn't want to talk about Kathleen, but he never even questioned why. Or *if.* Maybe his friend did want to talk about his loss.

Nathan went home and fell into a dreamless sleep. When he woke, he ambled into the front room, his thoughts still roiling.

Gene leaned back on the couch, staring at his computer screen. Nathan looked over his friend's shoulder and saw a blank document. "Writer's block?" he asked.

"Nah," Gene said. "My mind's not ready. It'll come."

Nathan poured a glass of water, then plopped down next to his friend. "You up for doing anything tonight?"

Gene frowned. "Like I said. I'm not in the mood."

"Not with Poppy."

He turned and met Nathan's eyes. "Yeah?"

"Just me and you."

Gene hummed and looked back at his computer screen. "Maybe. Gotta shake off this writer's block, I guess."

Nathan frowned. "You just said—"

"Yeah. Y'know. Whatever." Gene picked up his laptop and snapped it shut. "Let's go to Simon's."

It WAS NICE OUT, so they sat on the porch. Nathan ordered dinner for them both, waving off Gene's offer to split the bill. They inhaled mozzarella sticks and wings and sent off empty pint glasses to their blessedly patient server. Nathan reveled in the state of being unburdened. It was him, Gene, the warm breeze. The beer and the moment.

His phone vibrated, and he pulled it out of his pocket. Poppy's picture flashed on the screen.

Gene scowled. "You gonna answer it?"

"Nah." Nathan hit *ignore*. But it vibrated again, and he let out a heavy sigh. Gene rolled his eyes.

"Okay, I'll just talk to her for a minute." Nathan swiped at the green *answer* button. "Hey."

"Dude. You have to come over to Clever Girl." Poppy's voice was high-pitched, reedy. "Jen texted me. She's got the footage with Alicia from the other day."

Nathan got off his chair and stood up to pace. "She texted you?"

"Yeah, I slid her my number before we left." He could hear Poppy's grin on the other side of the line. "Might hook up later, I don't know."

Nathan gritted his teeth, his anger swelling. He'd never felt adrenaline course through his body like this. Instead of the butterflies that swirled in his stomach when Poppy spoke, he felt nothing but rage. He gripped the phone hard, and Gene stared at him with naked curiosity.

He let out a long breath. "Okay. Give me a little."

They Ubered across the city. Nathan worried that the entire fund his parents left him would be sucked up by Ubers and beers. Gene was unusually quiet.

They got out at the curb in front of the bar. It was raining, the kind of drizzle that could turn harder or slower any minute. Nathan raked a hand through his hair, already beaded with water.

The doors swallowed them in a mess of heat and sweat. Poppy sat at the bar, making googly eyes at Jen. Gene hung back as Nathan joined the two women. "What do you have?" he said dully.

Jen eyed him, as if he were a mere inconvenience. "I can't show you anything until we close. The camera feeds are in the back."

Nathan grunted. Gene wouldn't want to stay that long, and really, neither did he. Despite napping, he still felt terrible. He was ready to drop this "investigation" altogether. "Can't you get someone to cover?"

Jen snorted. "Because you work here?"

There were so many things he wanted to say. His mouth was so close to opening. But he balled his hands into fists, scraping his palms with his fingernails. "Listen, I'm on a deadline," he said. "Sorry if I sounded rude. I need to see that footage as soon as possible."

The bartender rolled her eyes.

Poppy turned to him. "Don't push it, Nathan. It's nice enough that Jen is helping us out with this. We're not police. She could get in trouble for showing this to us."

"What she said." Jen pointed to Poppy, who preened.

Nathan couldn't hold it in any longer.

"Why do you always do this, Poppy?" He leaned in, close enough that he could smell her breath, the cranberry mocktail lingering on her lips.

She pulled back. "Do what?"

"Manipulate people. Get them to want you so you can get what you want. Then turn them away."

Nathan heard a low whistle behind him. *Gene.* He kept going.

"You don't have a thing for Jen. Or Melissa the RA. Or me." He pointed a finger at her as a shocked expression spread across her face. "You're using us. You always have."

Poppy scowled, and her voice went dark. "How dare you."

"I've loved you for years." He was yelling now, drawing stares from the other patrons. "Every time you pretend to care about me, pretend I'm your boyfriend, you send me on this roller coaster. Why not just come out and say it? Tell me you only want to be friends. Tell Jen." Nathan motioned to the bartender, who was stock still.

Poppy stood up, put her hands on her hips. "I'm doing this for you. You're the one who started this whole thing. Trying to save the girls, like you're always trying to save everything. I went along with it because you wanted to be the white knight. The hero." She spat the last two words.

"You wanted to do this too." He wouldn't let her gaslight him. "You were there when we got the note from the Mothman."

The chatter around him slowed. Nathan went bright red, and Poppy's mouth dropped.

"Mothman?" someone yelled.

"Are you kidding? I love that guy!" someone else shouted.

The noise ramped back up. Nathan turned to look at Gene, and his friend shrugged.

Jen leaned over the bar. "Why didn't you say that? I'll take you back right now. I don't want to disappoint Mothman."

NATHAN AND POPPY stood stiffly around the computer as Jen pulled up the recording. Gene had stayed in the bar, smugly sipping another IPA.

The footage was clear, the technology up-to-date. The table in the corner looked just like that in Alicia's post. She leaned against the wall, her drink in hand, as a woman sitting across from her snapped a photo.

The two of them leaned together over a phone. There was no audio, but Nathan saw Alicia poking at the screen. He couldn't identify the other woman; she was a basic white girl, all legs and long blonde hair. Probably a pumpkin spice latte aficionado.

Then Poppy let out a short gasp.

"Oh. My. God," she said, one hand over her mouth and the other pointing at the computer.

Nathan's heart picked up its pace. "What?"

"Rewind that," she ordered. Jen tapped on her remote, which she controlled with her phone. The footage rewound. "Slow it down," Poppy said.

A face appeared on the women's phone screen. Nathan stared at it with unblinking shock.

"Fast-forward," Poppy barked. "I want to see her."

Nathan was shaking now. Jen sped through the images until the blonde girl moved her chair away from Alicia. They smiled at each other. Nathan could barely see the tilt of the blonde's face.

"We have to go back to the dorm."

Poppy grabbed his hand, but only a second passed before she dropped it.

"Where does she live?"

Poppy, Nathan, and Gene piled into the dorm's front lobby. The girl —*that* girl—was not at the front desk. Nathan hadn't seen anyone there since that first day.

"Hell if we know," Gene muttered.

"I have to find Melissa." Poppy whipped out her phone and started typing. "She needs to know."

Nathan and Gene huddled together behind their nearly manic friend. Nathan's heart had pounded the entire way back to the college. It was now close to midnight. People were already asleep. Poppy was going to wake up the whole dorm with her hysterics.

Poppy let out a breath and shoved her phone back into her pocket. "She's on her way down."

A minute went by. Five minutes. Poppy began to wring her hands. Fire was in Nathan's blood.

"Let's go upstairs," Poppy said.

They raced into the stairwell with its rubbery smell and the bulletin boards papered in college announcements. Gene hesitated at one of the landings, and Nathan gestured for him to hurry up. "One second," Gene said, and Nathan caught the ghost of an emotion flickering across his friend's face. Nathan hurried to catch Poppy as she burst out onto her floor.

Melissa's room was right at the end of the hall. Poppy began pounding on the door, loud and fast. "Melissa! Open up!"

No response.

Nathan grabbed the door and began rattling it. "We know you're in there!" he yelled.

He heard the doorknob jiggling, the metal slamming against the wood of the door.

Then the resistance fell away. The blonde girl from the front office stood in front of him. Her eyes were pools of brown. He noticed that her roots were sticking out above her platinum fall of hair.

"Nathan," she whispered.

Poppy blasted forward and shoved the blonde. But the other woman was strong; she wore a tank top, and her long ropy muscles were visible as she pushed Poppy back. Behind the tussle, Nathan spotted Melissa lying on the bed, unmoving, her face ashen.

"What did you do?" Poppy screamed.

The blonde stepped back, her chest heaving, blocking both of them from getting into the room. Nathan felt her stare on him like a spotlight.

"Please," she said. "I can explain."

"Gene! Gene! Where the fuck are you?" Poppy screeched.

Footsteps pounded up the stairs behind them. Gene got to the door just as Nathan elbowed Poppy out of the way. Nathan was right up next to the girl. "What is there to explain?" he said quietly.

The girl sagged against him.

He went still. Gene and Poppy, behind him, had quieted too. A handful of people still in the dorm peeked their heads out of their doors.

"You're right," she said. "I can't do this anymore."

Nathan had to lift her bodily in order to keep her standing. He didn't speak, just waited for her to talk. He couldn't see Poppy or Gene—just hoped that they were calling the police. And an ambulance for Melissa.

"Nathan, I'm crazy for you." The girl let out a long breath. "All I wanted was for you to notice me."

His thoughts ran circles in his mind. It was a wonder his brain hadn't fully broken. "But I don't know you."

"You never cared to. You've never even asked my name. All you ever do is run around after her. Poppy, Poppy, Poppy, she's all you think about. And then you showed up the other day with her..."

Nathan's mouth had gone dry. His arms were straining from holding her up. "What is your name?" he said carefully.

"Kennedy." She said it in a soft whimper. "I'm in three of your classes. And you don't even recognize me."

He sure did now. "I'm sorry, I..."

"I've tried to talk to you so many times. I thought... if she's out of the picture, things might be different. But I went about it all the wrong ways."

You're telling me, Nathan thought.

He couldn't hold her up anymore. She tumbled to the floor with a small shriek. The thunder of footsteps rumbled in the stairwell. Nathan stepped back as police and EMTs flooded the room.

"Nathan!"

In his dreams, his name was all he could hear. Kennedy whispering it. Poppy yelling it. His parents, his name on their dry lips as they passed one by one.

"Nathan." Someone was shaking him. "You've been asleep all day."

He blinked, rolled over. Poppy and Gene were standing above him. His bedroom was dark, but one window still had the shade rolled up. Outside, the sky was dusky, and flames crackled from the fire pit. Twinkle lights winked at him from the pergola.

"I could just sleep," he mumbled.

"You need to eat." Poppy reached out, then thought better of it. Gene grabbed Nathan's hand and pulled him out of bed. Together, the three friends piloted through the back door and out onto the patio.

For a while, they sat in silence, eating, watching the fire. Gene had put together turkey sandwiches with macaroni salad and chips, and there was ice cream for later. Nathan's head felt like a locked safe. The awkwardness in the air was palpable.

Finally, he thought of something to say. Nathan cleared his throat. "Did anyone hear from Mothman?"

They both shook their heads but seemed relieved for the tension to be somewhat broken. "There's just an article," Poppy said. "She confessed to everything. But it's a developing story."

Nathan set aside his plate—he'd vacuumed up the food. "I don't get it. Mothman said there were thirty souls. She would have killed that many people for me?"

Poppy held out her phone. She'd taken a picture of the original letter and peered down at it, pinching to zoom closer. "The letter says she was a true sociopath. Young in her career. Maybe she'd find out she really liked killing." Her voice lowered. "Maybe she would have liked killing me."

Neither he nor Gene could respond to that one.

Poppy was going home to her parents' for the evening. She needed space, she said, from campus and from Nathan and Gene. As she left, she put one hand on his arm and said she would text him.

Gene had put out the fire and cleaned up the plates.

"Thanks, man," Nathan said, huffing out a breath as he slumped onto the couch.

"Don't mention it." Gene took a seat next to him and powered on the XBOX.

"Surprised we haven't heard anything from Mothman yet," Nathan mused.

Gene shrugged. "Maybe he's done with us. He got what he wanted, right?" He paused with one hand on the controller, then met Nathan's eyes. "Did you?"

"The girls are okay," Nathan said. "The people Kennedy didn't kill... you know?"

"But with Poppy?"

Nathan shook his head. "I don't know about her."

∽

Nathan must have been tired, Gene thought, because he'd fallen asleep on the couch while Gene played *Call of Duty*. Gene himself felt somewhat numb. The whole thing had been a ridiculous affair, but then it became serious, and so much shit had stirred inside him. A series of wounds, ripped open between the three of them.

He thought he'd go to bed but wanted to make sure the fire was out first. He crept into the kitchen and eased out the back sliding door. The coals were all black, no embers left, and he was satisfied until he heard something. Wings flapping.

Gene blinked into the dark. "Hello?"

The porch light flicked on, and Gene startled. He hadn't touched anything. Was there a safety switch?

The little box sat on one of the Adirondack chairs around the fire.

He licked his lips and reached for it. Popped it open.

Eugene,

I know this has been a difficult time for you and your friends. I must say that I did not expect this. I knew that all three of you were affected by these tragedies, but I also knew you were the best detectives for the job. I thought the benefits would outweigh the risks to your personal psyches. I was wrong, and for that I apologize.

Yet I am impressed with your bravery. You set boundaries, chose to stay out of the picture when you needed to, and jumped in when you were needed. That's healthy, Eugene. Your behavior proves that you are capable of the next steps, even though they will be daunting.

The man who killed your sister is still out there. And we must find him before he kills again.

Gene dropped the letter into the fire pit. It didn't burn. He sank into a chair and watched it drift through the ash.

A PARTICULAR MELANCHOLY

Back in the nineties, if you wanted to start a band, you had to do it the old-fashioned way. Make flyers, stick them to bulletin boards. Haunt coffee houses and rundown bars. Figure out your sound: did you want that folksy singer with Farrah Fawcett hair or that funky emo guy with a mohawk? And how far would you go until you had the perfect combination?

A Particular Melancholy came together by the sheer determination of Phillip the Masked. Deenie was still in awe of him even after they'd been together as a band for more than a year. He was their lead singer and songwriter. He took them through rehearsals, booked gigs, yelled at Florence and Jack when they were at each other's throats. Deenie, Florence, Jack, and Hunter were only permitted to refer to him as Phillip the Masked, but Deenie called him Phil in her mind. It was shorter to say.

At first, Deenie didn't know why Phil was masked. He always wore black from head to toe: long T-shirt, jeans, heavy boots, even gloves. His head, too, was completely covered. Only his eyes peeked out from behind his ski mask. Deenie had asked Florence once what she thought, and Florence had only shrugged. "Musician," she explained.

PPHIL HAD FOUND Deenie on the street. Her parents' neighborhood had a summer festival thing every year, and she was playing with a pickup band there just for fun. It was her and a few guys she knew from high school. Deenie loved the drums: how she could wield the weight of those sticks in her hands. Slap the bass with her foot and clap the cymbals. Nothing drove her like a beat.

They were on the blacktop on one of the closed-off roads, facing an audience of neighbors on folding chairs. Halfway through the set, she noticed Phil under a tree, watching them. It kinda creeped her out—the hulking figure, clad head-to-toe in black—but Deenie was the kind of person who assumed the best of everyone. She worried that he was too hot and that he might need a glass of water.

He came up to her as she was disassembling her set. Deenie watched him approach. If it had been in the dark at night, she probably would have screamed and run away. But under the sizzling sun, he was only a curiosity.

She'd expected his voice to come out low and muffled, maybe even distorted, but it was high and clear. He was much taller than her, and he leaned down to shake her hand. When he introduced himself, she had to repress a snort. She kept her face neutral and let him keep talking. His band needed a drummer, and would she consider joining them?

Deenie did consider. She was a senior. She didn't know how old Phil was, but his bandmates, Florence and Jack, had already graduated from college. Her schedule—with band and extracurriculars and everything—was so packed. She didn't know where she would fit it all in.

Back then, you had to call each other. Cell phones were new and only rich people had them. Deenie remembered once when she'd gone to a birthday party in fifth grade. Her friend's mom had rented a limo for them, and they all thought they were so cool, sipping sparkling grape juice out of champagne glasses. The driver had a car phone. Imagine that—you could call people from your car. Whoa.

When Phil called, Deenie's mother answered the phone, and

Deenie cringed. Her mother sounded suspicious as she said, "Just a second," and handed the phone to Deenie.

"Have you thought about the band?" Phil asked, his voice melodic.

"Yeah," Deenie said.

Phil waited.

Deenie sighed. "What if I just sit in on rehearsal?"

"I still need a bass player. You know anyone?"

She did, actually. Hunter went to school with her and played double bass in orchestra. Scholarship kid, on to bigger and better things. She didn't think he'd be interested. "I'll ask him," Deenie said. "Even if just for rehearsal."

"I'd appreciate that." Phil did sound appreciative—almost relieved. "You free next Saturday?"

～

Deenie eventually learned that Phil had a skin disease. He was actually allergic to the sun. He even sounded apologetic when he said it, as if he was disappointing them. She felt so bad for him. In fact, she felt so bad for him all the time.

A Particular Melancholy started small. Phil was on lead vocal and rhythm guitar, with Jack on guitar and Florence on keyboard. Deenie could tell that the older band members were frustrated with her and Hunter's busy schedules. Jack and Florence sought fame and they wanted it fast.

They stuck together, though. Deenie and Hunter moved on to college, but they had time to perform in grungy bars at night. Sometimes they even got paid. Phil would dole out the cash at the end of the night, and Deenie would tuck it into a pocket inside one of her drum cases.

Word got around about the guy in the ski mask who sang so hauntingly. Whenever they played a slow ballad, Phil came alive. People in the audience wept as he clutched the mic, his guitar hanging loose. Usually these tunes featured only Phil and Florence, the piano soft under Phil's voice. Deenie would sit behind her set and let her gaze roam from Phil to the audience and back. He seemed to feed off their tears, pushing harder when their emotions swelled. Deenie would often choke up herself, even though she'd heard the songs a million times.

They leaned into their sound: a little bit folk, a little bit goth, with plenty of ballads for Phil. Soon they were playing bigger venues. They got a manager: Andie, cool and tattooed, her network wide. When Deenie graduated, she went right to recording their first EP.

BY THE SUMMER OF 2005, they'd been touring and recording albums for four years. They didn't know that their latest album, *Solid Stone,* would be their last.

After their shows, Phil would retreat to his single room. Deenie and Hunter had separate rooms within a suite, and Jack and Florence slept together, of course. Deenie thought about Phil all alone, shedding his black clothes, and felt like she could cry. Their next stop was Philadelphia, where Phil always struggled. He was from Pennsylvania, he said, and he always worried that his family would show up at their gigs. He'd grown up in the woods, near the Poconos, only a few hours' drive from the city.

Deenie's family had attended their show in Cleveland, and she was happy for it. Her parents had come around to her career, maybe because she was raking in the cash, and all of them lived comfortably now. She loved that they were there to cheer her on, but she hated that Phil had to be afraid of seeing his relatives. Deenie had lived such a charmed life that she couldn't understand how a family could fall apart.

Phil was quiet the entire trip. Deenie took a nap and rolled her eyes at Florence and Jack fighting over something stupid. Hunter had his headphones on and his eyes closed. Deenie knew Hunter was thinking about quitting the band to audition for symphony orchestras. The money was nice, he'd said, but playing on an orchestral stage was his dream. "We only have so much time," he told Deenie. "We won't be in our twenties forever."

That night, when Deenie entered the green room, Phil was absent. They'd already done sound check and set up their stuff; a large black curtain separated their equipment from the front of the stage, where the opener would perform. Florence was touching up her thick eyeliner while the other two men lounged on a red couch and picked at potato chips. Deenie wasn't worried until the opener came on.

As the folksy sound of a lone guitar filled the space, Andie popped in with a headset on. "Are we all ready?"

"We're not, actually." Florence stood with her hands on her hips, arms akimbo, black boots jangling with metal hardware. "Phil's not here."

Andie's eyes widened. "Where is he?"

"Fuck if we know," Jack said.

"Did anyone actually look?"

They shook their heads. Deenie felt dumb. She was past twenty-five now, but she still felt like a kid sometimes.

The search for Phil was brief and turned up nothing.

FLORENCE SANG THAT NIGHT. There was no rhythm guitar, but that was okay. Deenie held them together.

But the magic was missing. The audience loved them as usual, but the emotion that usually moved the crowd wasn't there. The applause felt halfhearted. Deenie left the stage feeling hollow. One of their puzzle pieces was missing.

A concert review came out the following day praising Florence's pinch-hit performance. She preened over it, announcing that she'd be happy to perform again at the next stop. Deenie told her bandmates that they couldn't leave until they found Phil, but Andie said no. They were booked for three more shows, and if he didn't show up, Florence would sing. Deenie thought about Phil's empty hotel room, a bed that wouldn't be unmade, a TV that wouldn't be turned on. No black clothes puddled on the floor.

~

In Boston, Florence and Jack made an announcement: they were leaving the band to start their own act. They'd be writing and performing folk together, and with their recent accolades, they had a jumping-off point. A Particular Melancholy crumbled just like that.

Katrina came. She wreaked havoc on Louisiana, but the Midwest only got rain: buckets of it. Deenie retreated to her Cleveland apartment, sitting on her savings and wondering what she would do next. Drummers didn't really do solo acts. Dave Grohl didn't count because he started an entirely new band. She'd have to find another band to join. Either that or take on an entirely different career. What would she do, become an actuary? A paralegal? She wasn't qualified for anything. And she wanted nothing but to sit behind those drums.

One night, she lay in bed listening to the rain pummel her windows. She kept thinking about all those people who lost their lives, their livelihoods, their possessions. Deenie felt sadness from everywhere, permeating her bedroom and sneaking into her soul. She wished for Phil to come back, but she knew he never would. She would have to find him.

Deenie jumped up and started her computer, then proceeded to scour the Internet for information about the Poconos. It's hard to believe, but back then there weren't even smartphones. If you were tech-savvy, you might have a computer in your apartment and even a broadband connection. She was lucky to have the money for such things, even though her first PC was loaded with malware because she didn't know about antivirus scanners.

She noodled around for a while, searching for different lodgings and activities in the mountains. It was such a huge region with so much to do. So many places Phil could hide. And he'd never given them many details about his life, let alone anything specific about where he'd lived growing up. Deenie felt a sudden hunger to know—and a sudden sting because she'd never thought to ask.

Deenie got up for a glass of water, then re-settled in her seat. She forced herself to think. Then she typed *A Particular Melancholy Poconos, Pennsylvania.*

Google links spread before her in a line of blue results. The first thing that came up was a forum dedicated to the group. Deenie blinked at the site, her eyes still sore from looking at the bright monitor in the darkness. This was a website entirely devoted to people talking about their band. *Her* band.

Well, it had been theirs.

As she scrolled through the threads, her heart started hammering. There were all sorts of topics that turned her stomach. One entire thread was about her; when she clicked on it, she nearly screamed in disgust. So many posts were dedicated to shipping them—drawing, writing, fantasizing about Deenie having sex with everyone and anyone in her band. Including Andie. *Yuck.*

She clicked away and scrolled down, looking for more valuable information. Her heart picked up speed as she noticed a thread titled *Phillip sighting?*

Does anyone know where Phillip is from? I was camping out near Stroudsburg and my friends were playing the Solid Stone *CD. We started seeing this guy skulking around. Thought it might have been a bear or even a Bigfoot. But then we saw it was a guy all in black. Really looked like him. Super weird.*

Commenters had responded.

There was a story in Entertainment Weekly *about the band starting in Ohio? I don't know anything about Pennsylvania.*

I was at the show in Philly a couple years ago and he mentioned he was from there.

Dude I was at that show. Is there a bootleg of it?

Yeah, we gotta confirm this.

Anyone else camp out there? Try playing the album? I'm all the way in Indy. OP, you might have to go back out there.

I'm the leader of a fan club out here in Pittsburgh. Still a bit of a drive, but might be fun. I'll ask if anyone wants to do an outing.

She swallowed. Her fingers shook as she created an account and navigated to the thread. Clicked the button to add a new post and typed, *Where exactly were you when you saw him? I can go.*

~

DEENIE LEFT Ohio on the first of October and found a hotel in Stroudsburg.

When she checked in, no one recognized her. Deenie supposed drummers always faded into the background. She sat in the lobby, people-watching, wondering where she might pick up a clue. Back then, wireless internet was not as readily available, and smartphones were nonexistent. She would have to ask around.

"I'm looking for my friend," Deenie said, leaning over the hotel bar. She'd put on a low-cut shirt. Did her makeup in sultry shadows. Deenie knew she was pretty, even more so when she went totally goth. Her skin was ivory-pale, her hair dyed black—catnip for metalheads.

The bartender that night warmed to her right away. "Yeah? Got any more details than that?"

"We were in a band together." Deenie sat back and played with a strand of hair. "A Particular Melancholy?"

"Shit. You were in that band? Crazy what happened to them... you?"

The bartender was a big guy, built nicely, white but not pale. Big gauges in both ears, brown hair, chain on his belt. He grinned at Deenie, looking like he wanted to eat her for dinner. Actually, Deenie did want dinner, so she ordered a burger. The guy hopped to it, bringing her a glass of red wine on the house.

"I'm Harrison," the bartender said as Deenie sipped her wine and waited for her burger. "You're the drummer, huh."

"Process of elimination?" she asked.

He flushed.

"It's okay. You can't really see me from the audience. I'm hidden behind all that other equipment." She flashed a grin, then let her face relax. "In all seriousness. My friend Phil, you remember?"

"Phillip the Masked? Who could forget." Harrison whistled. "He was something. But the most beautiful voice I've ever heard on a guy. Soulful. Couldn't help crying anytime I saw you play."

"So yeah, he disappeared when we played here this summer," Deenie said.

Harrison held up a finger. "Hold that thought. Your food's up."

She rested her chin on her hand as she waited.

He returned with her plate, napkins, condiments. Deenie hadn't realized how hungry she was. She started cutting her burger in half. Harrison held up a hand. "I can get that for you."

"It's okay." She'd already cut it all the way down. "You were saying you knew something about Phillip?"

"I can't say I know anything for sure..." Harrison trailed off.

Deenie winked. "Don't bartenders know everything?"

He laughed. "I certainly don't."

She started on half the burger. It was so good.

Harrison lay tangled in her sheets, snoring lightly. Deenie lay propped on her elbow, admiring him. He was easy to look at. Tattoos of the Greek alphabet circled his muscled chest, and she wondered what their significance was.

When her arm fell asleep, she flopped onto her back and stared at the ceiling.

Harrison said some of the staff had observed Phil leaving the hotel and hiking up the mountain behind it. There were mountains everywhere in Pennsylvania, nothing like the flat expanses of her home state. Deenie pictured it, the steep incline. Not a chance she could get up there.

When Harrison woke up, he grabbed her around the waist and pulled her close. "I can't believe I've been with a celebrity," he whispered, breath hot against her ear.

Deenie adjusted herself so he could hold her more comfortably.

"I wouldn't call myself a celebrity."

He tapped her lightly on the nose. "You know, I do play some guitar."

Of course he did. "I suppose you're going to ask me when we can start a band."

His smile tipped just slightly. "Nah. I like you, Deenie. I don't wanna take advantage of you."

She was taking advantage of him. But she did think it would be fun.

"What if I wanted you to play with me?"

His grin widened. "Didn't I play with you enough last night?"

"Silly." She was next to boop him on the nose. "I mean jam together. Would your boss let you do that? Maybe on the patio tonight. With the fires going?"

Harrison sat up straight and stared her right in the eyes. "Are you kidding? You would do that?"

Deenie reached for his hands. "Dead serious."

DEENIE DIDN'T GO ANYWHERE without a drum set. Granted, it was one of her cheaper kits, but still. One never knew when there would be an opportunity to play, and this was it.

She and Harrison fell into an easy rhythm. Following him was effortless. She liked the way he swayed when he sang, bending the guitar back and forth on his hips.

An audience gathered. She suspected most of them knew the bartender better than they knew Deenie, but it was nice all the same. She'd missed the small gigs, where she could see everyone's faces, where there were no stage lights blasting her in the eyes. The smattering of applause felt like music on its own.

The night got deeper and chillier, but the fire pits kept the hotel guests warm. She wasn't sure how long Harrison would want to play. But she was hoping her ploy to draw Phil out had already worked.

Finally, Harrison announced that this would be their last tune, and

Deenie heard a rustling noise behind her. She sat up a bit on her stool and turned toward the edge of the trees behind the hotel. A dark figure was veiled among the brush, and even though she couldn't see its eyes, she could tell it was watching her.

As she and Harrison packed up, he looked down on her with a pleased expression. "That was really cool," he said.

"Totally." Deenie stood and let him pull her toward him. "We should do it again."

"Isn't there something else we should do again?"

"Totally," she said again, then bowed her head to fit into the spot between his neck and chest. "But I think I saw Phil. Phillip, I mean. Watching us."

Harrison rubbed her back. He smelled so good—whatever deodorant or scent he wore carried her away to some ocean. "I'm guessing you want to talk to him?"

"Yeah. But here's my key." She reached in her back pocket and handed it to him. "I'll meet you up there, okay?"

"Okay," he said. "I'll take your set up."

Deenie stepped away and put her hands together in thanks. Then she backed off. There wasn't time to chase the butterflies in her stomach.

SHE PICKED her way through the grass until the terrain began to slope upward.

"Phil!" she yelled. "I know you're here."

Deenie was not a mountain goat. She wouldn't get much further. "Phil!" she yelled again. "You can at least show your face."

Too late she realized that it was the wrong thing to say.

A creature raised its head out of the brush. She drew in a gasp as she took in its appearance. A chilly wind dragged across her arms and shoulders, and she shivered even in her down jacket.

Deenie started to shake. Tears pooled in her eyes.

The creature's skin folded in on itself dozens of times. The flaps accordioned down its back, on its belly, along its fat tail. The Michelin man taken to a slimy extreme. Deenie's jaw hung loose. Cold air scraped along her throat; those tears dripped down her cheeks.

As she sobbed, the creature stood. It grew taller, the tail separating into legs, but it only had a vaguely human shape. Deenie pressed her face into her hands.

"It's Phillip the Masked," Phil said.

Deenie's voice was hoarse. "You're not masked."

"Not right now, no."

Phil's face was permanently sad. His beady black eyes peered out from between his bloated cheeks and forehead.

Deenie clasped her hands together, pushing them so hard her wrists could break. "Why did you leave?"

"It was getting too much," he said. "Making sure I had enough sorrow to survive."

She blinked and huddled closer inside her coat. Phil stepped back further into the shadows. It was harder to make out his features. Those strange features she'd always wanted to see, finally exposed. "You said you never wanted to come back here. To your family."

"I didn't." He shook his head, the gesture melting into the dark. "But it was inevitable, Deenie. I couldn't keep up the ruse. Not even for all the sadness in the world."

She understood then. He fed on their emotions. His voice made the tears come. His every move was to exploit them—their audience—their future.

Part of her wanted to scream. To rage in his face for using them. For abandoning them when they needed it most. But the other part just mourned. For what Phil was. For what he could have been.

He began to falter, stumbling even further, his legs collapsing. She couldn't see him anymore. His voice came, keening into the night, that high and mournful melody that had stolen everyone's breath and tears.

Deenie returned to the hotel with something wrong inside her. She melted into Harrison, let his distractions take her away, but she was aimless. Half there and half somewhere in the Alleghenies.

She gave Harrison her number. Unlimited talk was only after nine and he was usually working. But they stole moments here and there. She'd begun to like him—she really had. Yet what they were doing was like a bud, a flower that couldn't bloom.

Deenie let this hang over her for a few years. Florence got pregnant twice and split with Jack. Hunter became principal bass in the Seattle Symphony. Deenie joined a band that played gigs in the bars A Particular Melancholy used to haunt. The ones with smoke still clinging to their wooden walls and tables. She got a job as a part-time barista for the health insurance.

One day she was on the couch flipping channels when she stopped hard on the public access channel. The person onscreen was covered in black from head to toe, only those beady eyes peering out. He sang with a soaring orchestra behind him, his voice booming into the rafters. So confident. Soaking it all up as the audience swooned.

She could have been angry. She could have tracked him down and screamed at him about how he betrayed them. Deenie had him to blame for her entire life.

But she also had him to thank. And she let that live inside her as she watched him looming large on the screen. And she let the tears flow.

VANISHING TWIN SYNDROME

Notes of Dr. Leslie Kravitz

March 8, 2028

Patient: 28yo pregnant with twins. Name: Marianna Campbell. White/Caucasian. About four months, preparing for anatomy scan at 20 weeks. Have scheduled sugar test for 27 weeks. Overall healthy, babies' heartbeats sound good. Will see again at ultrasound.

March 21, 2028

9am Marianna Campbell. I've never seen anything like this outside of a medical textbook. Twins are conjoined at the head. Referred to team at the specialty surgery center in Philadelphia.

Leslie's Diary

March 21, 2028

I seriously cannot believe what happened at work today. I tried to tell Dave about it, but he didn't feel like talking. I know his job has been stressful, and I try to respect that, but how could he not want to hear about this? It's exciting and scary all at the same time.

I feel bad for the patient. She was nervous about having twins in the first place. I had to give her the bad news. I thought her eyes would fall out of her head. Her hands started shaking. I placed my palm over her hand, hoping to calm her, but she jerked her hand away. I was surprised but understood. Not everyone likes to be touched, and I wouldn't normally touch a patient, but I was so worried. I still am.

Notes of Dr. Leslie Kravitz

March 26, 2028

Marianna Campbell was sent to the Center for Fetal Diagnosis and Treatment immediately after I reviewed my findings. Full day of scans to confirm my initial diagnosis. The team at the hospital set up a session with me to discuss the care plan.

Craniopagus twins, as I suspected. The team recommends she transfer to the specialty birthing center at 28 weeks. I will be on site periodically and present at delivery.

Leslie's Diary

March 26, 2028

I can't help it. I'm lonely.

I don't know what to do about my marriage. Dave is so distant. His nose is already stuck to his phone screen. He doesn't even play video games anymore. When he's not working, he's doomscrolling. I shouldn't rely on him for constant company—it isn't fair to him—but he never wants to talk to me. I'm rarely home, I don't have friends, and I don't have any connections other than those at work. I put on a big smile when I'm working with patients and at the hospital delivering, but at home I'm deep in the dumps. Half the time I'm too tired to even pursue a hobby or read.

Notes of Dr. Leslie Kravitz

March 30, 2028

Reviewed the care plan with the team at CFDT onsite. The focus now is on safe delivery. After birth and aftercare of the patient, my responsibilities will end, but we reviewed the post-birth activities for my information. The babies will receive a comprehensive analysis for potential surgery. Craniopagus twins have been successfully separated, most recently at UC Davis (CA), although even specialty surgeons may have never encountered these cases. They account for only two percent of conjoined twin cases worldwide. We will continue to meet regarding patient's scheduled C-section, length of gestation, and bed rest.

Leslie's Diary

April 2, 2028

Marianna showed up at the clinic today. She didn't have an appointment, but the team at the front desk knows she's a special patient. Noreen poked her head into my office and whispered, "You have a visitor."

I looked up from my laptop. I'd been reviewing charts, and my back hurt from hunching over the keyboard. I needed a stretch anyway. "Who is it?"

Noreen's whisper was almost a hiss. "Marianna Campbell."

I couldn't help feeling a little excited. Since she went to the specialty center, I've been feeling left out. I'm a boring old OB-GYN who can't do anything but catch babies and do pap smears. I know that's not true—I didn't go through the hell of internship and residency for nothing—but after years of the same-old, same-old, I've become an island.

I went out to the front to meet her. Marianna was drained and pale. She wore a stained, light blue fleece coat, and her arms were wrapped protectively over her belly. Her brown hair was limp, her face inflamed with acne.

"Are you okay? Do we need to get you in for an emergency appointment?" I stepped toward her, then thought better of myself. I'd almost touched her shoulder in front of other patients, who were already turning our way.

"No." Her voice was soft. "Can I talk to you?"

I ushered her back into my office. The laptop's bright screen was too harsh against the dusky room. I closed it and flipped on the warm lamp at my desk. "What's wrong?"

Marianna fidgeted. Her hands were scraped raw and bloody from too much picking at her skin. "Something is wrong with the babies."

I nearly jumped out of my seat. "You said—"

"I don't need an appointment." She pinched her lips, which made her look even more skeletal. "This is inside. Nothing you will find on an ultrasound."

I noticed, for the first time, that she had the hint of an accent. Eastern European. She must have married into her last name. She'd always been so quiet in my exam room. Short, clipped, yet soft responses to my questions. It struck me then—Marianna was more than a patient. She had an ocean inside her. Not just two babies, but multiples of herself. She hadn't shared that with anyone, and I felt privileged to know.

"Then tell me." I lowered my voice to match hers. "What can I do to help you?"

She paused, touched her belly. "One girl is going away."

"What do you mean?"

"Leaving. Disappearing."

It wasn't unheard of. Vanishing twin syndrome—where one twin takes more of the mother's resources, and the other is never even detected. Still, this was unlikely so far into her pregnancy, especially in a case of conjoined twins. I tried not to speak from my doctor brain when I replied, but before I could say anything, she continued. She must have seen the puzzlement on my face.

"I know you don't understand. It's okay. I mean, I will not be okay, but..." She leaned forward and closed her eyes, massaged the skin at her temples. "This is something that happens. I wanted you to prepare."

"Marianna." I couldn't help myself—I placed a hand on her knee. "You need water and something to eat. Can I take you to get a bite?"

She shook her head violently. "No, no... I shouldn't have come. I knew you would not understand."

Marianna struggled to get to her feet. I grabbed her hands to steady her. "I want to understand," I said. "How can I learn?"

She pointed to my desk, and I followed her finger to a notepad that read *ACOG 2024*. I handed it to her, along with a pen. She scribbled while I rummaged in my desk. We turned at the same time. She handed me the notepad, and I pressed a protein bar into her hands in return.

I escorted her back outside. It was hard to watch her go, looking so lonely, but I promised myself I'd follow up. I'd do whatever I could to help. That was why I became a doctor in the first place.

THE HOUSE WAS empty when I got home. I spooned up some cold pasta salad and ate it in front of my laptop. I didn't even turn up the heat.

Marianna had written one word. *Strzyga.* Enough for me to Google. Enough for me to bristle at the search results.

The strzyga were born from an ancient Polish legend: vampire twins who devour each other. One twin eventually takes over, but at a price. Crazed with rage at losing her sister, her bloodlust drives her mad. She can never get enough blood.

I'm squirming as I write this now. I'm in bed. I've written this much because I need to process it all. All these strange revelations. In the legend, these strzyga are grown women. Sometimes they even look like shrieking, evil owls. How could a baby destroy another?

Notes of Dr. Leslie Kravitz

April 9, 2028

Met with practitioners and patient regarding 27-week sugar test. Dr.

Terrence at CFDT is concerned about patient's weight, as am I. The test may put her sugars into an abnormal range. Tested with blood pricks—patient did not tolerate well.

Leslie's Diary

I'm even more worried about Marianna after today.

Dr. Terrence administered a finger prick to test her A1C—a measure of the sugar in her blood over time. I'd thought she understood there'd be a needle. But she freaked when the blood bubbled up on her finger. She shoved it into her mouth and sucked on it. Her face was as pale as I'd ever seen it.

She got up and paced the room. The specialists were all over her, asking if they could give her something to calm her down—pregnancy-safe, of course. She pushed them away, gnashing her teeth. I stood in the corner, crossing my arms.

"Dr. Kravitz!" someone yelled.

Marianna turned back to me. We locked eyes, and she quieted. "I'll get you a glass of water," I said and saw myself out.

When I returned, my patient was back on the table, sitting up, her chest heaving. I handed her the water—I'd purchased a cold bottle from a vending machine.

"Well, she's all done." Dr. Terrence said, speaking like Marianna wasn't even there. "We have some concerns."

I turned back to look at Marianna, but she wasn't paying attention. She was sipping the water, staring into the middle distance. Sweat beaded on her brow.

"The reaction being foremost." Dr. Hale frowned and tapped a pencil against her teeth. "But the heartbeat scan was also not great."

I tipped my head.

"Both babies are healthy. I don't see the need for another scan today." Dr. Terrence glanced back at Marianna. "She was so agitated. She flailed, almost knocked the wand out of my hand."

"We may need to consider some supplements to her care," Dr. Hale said. "Psychiatry, specifically."

I gritted my teeth. As if I didn't know we were talking about our patient's mental health.

We left the room while she got dressed. When she emerged, Marianna looked defeated, but at least she was upright. I escorted her out and stood next to her as she scheduled her next appointment. Then I followed her into the hallway. "I don't feel good about you driving home," I told her.

"I don't drive," she said. "My husband will pick me up."

She'd never mentioned a husband, nor had he come with her to any appointments.

A nurse barreled past, and we stepped aside. I ushered Marianna into the elevator, guiding her by an elbow. Her bones were like a bird's. "When will he be here?" I asked.

She leaned against the elevator's back rail. I have always hated the glass walls in this hospital. It felt as if one of us could plummet to the atrium floor at any moment.

"Let me drive you home," I said.

I needed to get back to the office to see other patients, but I couldn't help scoping out Marianna's neighborhood. Small, cute houses lined up in a neat row on a suburban street. I was relieved to see that her bungalow was well-kept, the garden weed-free, grass trimmed. Flowers would bloom soon. I feel like a snob even saying this, but the area seemed safe. Marianna doesn't need any more stress.

Before I left her driveway, I scrawled my cell number on an old receipt and stuck it in her purse. "Please call me," I said. "If you need anything."

Dave was home this afternoon. He didn't react when I slung my purse on the counter or when my keys jingled in the door, only mumbled hello when I acknowledged him. I went upstairs to write this. Next I'll run a bath and go to bed early. I have call tomorrow night, so it's best to be rested. I suppose Marianna and I are the same way in one regard—we both have vanishing husbands.

Notes of Dr. Leslie Kravitz

April 6, 2028

Marianna Campbell is no longer under my care. I wish her well with her new care providers. Her notes will remain in her electronic chart to be transferred. Her doctors at the specialty clinic were chagrined. I too feel a sense of disappointment at the close of the file.

Leslie's Diary

Marianna called me after her 28-week appointment, which I did not attend, as I was seeing patients in the office that day. I didn't know it was her, so I let it go to voicemail. She hung up before leaving a message.

When I got back to my desk, she'd left me a text. *Please call now.* No preamble, no instructions. I called her at the end of my shift. Despite my fears for Marianna, the other patients were still my responsibility.

She answered. Her voice was quiet, but there was a hint of steel behind it I'd never noticed before. "I left the specialty center," she said.

"What?" I was still in my office, bent over my desk, my head in my hands. The office staff were already gone, and the place was eerily quiet. Irrationally, I was thinking about all the patients who'd suffered here through the years. This place wasn't all happiness and sunshine. How could I have dismissed my job as rote when I was making referrals to oncologists and helping patients heal from child loss? A single bolt of anger went through my chest, and I gripped the phone.

"They wanted to deliver today."

"At 28 weeks?" I woke my laptop and keyed in my password. "Have there been more complications? My notes say you were supposed to stay there but not necessarily deliver."

"The second baby is gone," Marianna said, matter-of-fact. "Now things will be different. I will need you to care for me at my home."

I frowned as I pulled up her chart. How bold of her to assume I would put my license in danger like that. I let the silence stretch as I read through

Dr. Terrence's notes. They'd wanted to perform emergency surgery after losing the heartbeat of Baby B, which is what I would have done. The dead tissue could endanger Baby A. I said as much to Marianna.

"You are as ignorant as they are, Dr. Kravitz. I thought better of you." There was a sneer in her voice. "I am the one carrying a demon inside me."

I sat up. Prepartum psychosis? Some other psychiatric ailment? As attached as I'd let myself get—I didn't know this woman at all.

"She'll absorb the other twin," Marianna continued. "But I'll need to deliver her as soon as that's done, or else she'll start devouring me from the inside."

A headache had grown beside my temple. I massaged both sides, willing my sinuses to drain. "If you knew this would happen, why seek conventional treatment at all?"

"I was stupid." Her voice cracked. "Too hopeful."

The sun was near setting. I flipped on my desk lamp. Was there a chance this wasn't an entire hallucination from an addled, hormonal mind? Could I put aside science for this?

I shut down the laptop. "When did you know?"

A long pause. Then, "I hoped I was wrong. But when they were conjoined... That's usually how it starts."

My heart cracked. I wondered if she had been vibrant and dynamic before, a ball-buster lawyer or exec. Hollowed out from within by a legend thousands of years older than modern medicine. Knowing two babies would become one.

"Okay. Let me think." It was hard to puzzle this out with pain thumping above my eyes. "What do you want?"

"I said, I'd like you to care for me at my home. Money isn't an object. Stanley has plenty."

"I'm sorry. I don't think I can. Even if I could, we'd both have to sign a contract." Did my malpractice insurance cover supernatural complications?

She blew out a breath. "Fine. I will engage with a midwife in the community. Goodbye, Dr. Kravitz. You've been helpful."

"Wait!" I couldn't let this end now. "Have your midwife list me at the doctor on record. I'd like her to call me if there are any issues."

"No need. This will be taken care of."

The call ended. A solid ball of anxiety had formed in my gut. A blank, empty feeling coated my brain. I opened the laptop, tapped in my final notes, and left the office.

Leslie's Diary / Patient Log

Tonight has been... wow. Well, last night, I suppose. I've been awake for almost 48 hours. My head is spinning.

The last few weeks have been awful. I put on a smile for my patients and colleagues, but inside it felt like I'd been scooped out. Become a husk of myself. Moving through life with a mask on.

Yesterday afternoon, a call came from her number. I considered ignoring it, but that wouldn't be right. I couldn't let my bruised ego get away with her safety, even if she was no longer my patient.

The smooth voice on the other end took me by surprise. "Dr. Kravitz—my name is Anya Villeneuve. I'm working with Marianna Campbell. She's requested you."

I forced my voice to cool. "She is no longer my patient."

"You're listed as the doctor on record."

I swallowed. "Okay. What complication are we looking at?"

"Does there need to be one?" The midwife lowered her voice. "She's scared."

I couldn't get there fast enough.

Marianna was wearing an oversized tee with no pants. She lumbered from side to side, groaning. A plastic tarp covered the carpet. Her living room was as quaint as her home, minimal, with two over-stuffed couches and tasteful artwork. A single framed photo on a sideboard pictured Marianna with her husband. He was tall, brawny, barrel-chested, but he had an impish smile.

Anya caught me staring at the portrait. "He's at work. Says he's finishing up and coming home."

Marianna lifted her head. Our eyes met, and my stomach tingled.

She gave me a tired smile, and I relaxed. Maybe we could put all the weirdness aside. Or at least that was what I thought until the labor ramped up.

She moaned and circled the floor. When I arrived, her contractions were hard but slow. Now there was no gap between them. As much as I wanted to help, I knew I couldn't. This was beyond me.

Marianna screamed. Her pain cut through me.

"Can you push?" Anya asked softly.

"Not... time." Marianna clenched her jaw.

"I don't know if he'll get here in time," Anya soothed. "The baby could hurt you if you wait."

Marianna looked stricken. She was drenched in sweat. The skin of her belly undulated as the creature within her writhed. Despite my terror, I'd been through worse medical situations. I had to put my feelings in a box on the top shelf of my mental closet. I exchanged a glance with Anya.

"She needs to move along," Anya said softly.

I cleared my throat. "So she's not progressing?"

Marianna looked at me as if finally seeing me for who I was. "I'm not going back to the hospital. I wanted you here. Not in any office. I finally accepted—" She broke into another scream. "My daughter will be born violent."

"We need to get her out somehow, then." Anya stepped toward Marianna and motioned for me to follow. "I'll massage your pelvis. Dr. Kravitz will stay up front to catch her. You focus on pushing. You're fully dilated now. We'll do this together."

I moved awkwardly in front of Marianna. She smelled of blood and sweat. Her eyes were bloodshot as well, like she'd pushed her eyeballs out of her head. "I don't know what to do," she cried.

"Shh. Relax." I moved my hands along her arms. "I know it's hard. You can do it."

With the first push, I could see the head peek out, then retreat. This was normal, as the birth canal would stretch and spread to make way for the whole body. But as I eased the baby out of Marianna's crouching body, I saw its face and screamed.

It had teeth. Huge, gleaming, sharp teeth. I've heard of infants being born with teeth, but never like this. Never such a vicious appetite from such a helpless creature. This baby wasn't a baby. It was a demon.

It flailed and roared. Covered with vernix and coated in blood, it appeared unholy. Marianna grimaced and lurched forward to take her from my trembling hands. She shoved her wrist up to its face, and it drank.

The baby was insatiable. Anya and I both offered our wrists. It was a sweet sting, followed by a euphoric head rush. I cradled the baby while she drank until I got woozy. I thought she'd bleed us all dry until she finally relaxed into sleep.

Marianna cleaned herself up. Anya disposed of the tarp. I was alone holding the baby when the front door rattled open and the brawny man from the photo walked in. "What'd I miss?" His eyes caught on the baby resting in my arms. "She's here?"

I handed the snoozing child-demon to her father. He flashed his broad, flat teeth and jostled her in his arms. She woke and turned toward him, nipping at his skin. To my surprise, he was nonplussed as the baby sank her teeth into his wrist. I watched the way he looked at his daughter—like she hung the moon—and I thought suddenly of her twin.

When I got home tonight, I told Dave I was leaving him.

A *STRYGKA IS* bent on revenge. She is mild-mannered until she loses her other half—only then does rage consume her. And the bloodlust takes over. Lilinka will not be like other little girls. She will be feral, uncaged. She will be dangerous.

I moved my things into an apartment. Dave and I pursued a swift no-fault divorce. We shook hands at the courthouse, the same one where we'd married fourteen years ago. When I'd thought a stable, boring relationship would fulfill me as I completed medical school. Now, when I saw that baby, saw her lustiness and passion, a fire sparked in me. Dave and I should have never married. But I could still break myself from him.

I was settling into my new apartment, sprucing up the space, letting light pour into the windows on a sunny spring morning. I'd put coffee on and let myself savor the scent as I breezed onto my porch. I felt so light. Fully human. A part of me had withered and died, subsumed by the life that now thrummed through me.

GUESS WHO'S COMING TO DINNER

Mrs. Quatch ushered Minnie's family through the front door. *Oh, good*, she thought. Her sister had brought dessert. Mrs. Quatch wouldn't have to crack open the Marie Callender's pie she'd bought in case of emergency. Her sister wasn't always very reliable. But today, they'd arrived on time and with the appropriate items. She could have kissed Minnie but instead wrapped her in a tight hug.

Minnie laughed and stroked Mrs. Quatch's back fur. It felt nice. Like Mrs. Quatch was appreciated.

Her nephews went flying down into the basement, no doubt looking for the old gaming system that collected dust there.

The adults headed into the kitchen. Minnie's husband Gordon hugged Michael and slapped his back. Mrs. Quatch beamed. Her teenager, Agatha, served the family warm apple cider out of tiny cups. Everyone laughed and noted, as they always did, that more items should be right-sized for them.

"Humans are so stubborn." Michael shook his head and blew on the drink. "We're second-class to them. They can't admit there should be an infrastructure in place for us too."

"Their civilization isn't built for us," Gordon pointed out. "We don't need their social benefits. Look what we've done without them. Look at this house!" He gestured to the festive living room, all decked out with tinsel and lights.

"We never dreamed of indoor plumbing and soft beds. We've grown spoiled," Michael growled. "They owe us more than that."

Mrs. Quatch tensed. The last thing they needed was another political estrangement in the family. Soon there would be no one left. She really did love Gordon—he was the only constant in her life, from their time in the woods to this beautiful house. But she had lost so much because of her husband's stubbornness.

There was a crash from downstairs, and Minnie sighed.

"Don't get up." Mrs. Squatch flapped a hand at her sister. "They'll be fine."

Gordon tipped his head at her. "Anyone else coming? The Widefoots?"

Mrs. Quatch shook her head. "They're traveling. Agatha is feeding their cats."

Agatha smoothed her fur. "I'm so jealous. They've got such lovely coats."

"You know your father's allergic." Mrs. Quatch clicked her tongue. "You can visit the Widefoots anytime."

Agatha stuck out her tongue. "But their kids are so gross! Their room is rank. I don't think they ever wash their fur."

Michael fixed her with a look. "Does your mother need any help with dinner?"

Agatha took the hint and followed Mrs. Quatch into the kitchen. They began arranging the dishes on the island. A small buffet awaited them: two huge cooled birds, a vat of potatoes, Minnie's sizable pie. Much more appropriate than the backups Mrs. Quatch had bought. Gordon could eat that frozen pie all by himself. What had she been thinking? God bless Minnie. Now the meal would be perfect.

Just in time, the oven beeped, and Mrs. Quatch removed seven golden loaves of French bread from the oven. She set out seven sticks of butter and surveyed her handiwork.

Agatha frowned and rolled her eyes. "Mom. We're supposed to be watching carbs."

"What do you think potatoes and pumpkin pie are?" Mrs. Quatch laughed. "Your father will be fine for one day."

Her daughter frowned. "You know what happens when we get diabetes? He could lose a foot."

There came a stampede from the basement as the boys emerged. Liam and Louis—twins, they'd been nearly the death of Minnie. Their kind didn't take well to multiple births.

"What did you say?" Liam crowed. "That Agatha's an idiot?"

"Quit it, nerd-brain!" Agatha snapped back. "Don't let your fur get wet when some popular human kid sticks your head in the toilet."

"Oddly specific insult," Louis murmured.

Liam elbowed his brother. "Those human kids are mean."

"Everyone stop it!" Mrs. Quatch held up her palm. "This is supposed to be a nice family dinner."

And that was when the doorbell rang.

It had taken every fiber of Peter's being to travel cross-country. He blamed Seneca, his new wife, who insisted on meeting his family. "We're estranged," Peter pointed out over and over as their disagreement dragged on. "The two of us can have a nice holiday here."

"We didn't have a wedding." Seneca clapped her hands together and interlaced her fingers. "Please?"

He'd eyed her, his stomach churning, and he had to race to the bathroom. When he returned, she looked sad. "I'm sorry," she said. "I should know better. We'll have our own Thanksgiving."

Peter sighed. She reached for him, her wide palm smoothing the hair on his legs, and Peter thought of his mother. Her stricken face when he told her he was leaving town. Peter and his father wouldn't speak again after the argument they'd had, after Peter's father had slammed him into the ground as if he were still a child.

Seneca knew all this. Peter supposed she too could see the image of his mother behind her eyes. Her own mother had died young, and she was still filled with rage. He wondered if that was why Seneca wanted to meet his mother so badly. She had no one else besides him.

Now they sat in the truck, parked outside the house, deep in Michigan's upper peninsula. They had driven for days. Peter was exhausted. Seneca should have let him call first. He hoped that after this, she would let the matter of his family be. He loved the life they had. He'd picked up a job at a bar on the reservation, and she was working the tables. They connected over their shared love of literature and learning. Seneca was passionate about cryptid rights, and Peter had left his family over them.

She opened the passenger door. "Let's go in."

He almost stopped her even after the long journey. Maybe watching from the window would mollify her. Maybe she should knock and he could stay outside. He'd do anything to not feel like being eaten from the inside.

Mrs. Quatch's stomach swooped at the sight of her son.

It had been three years. Three long years with no contact. Her boy's face was like a bright light. The mother she was once, holding her first baby to her breast, took her back in time in an instant.

She reached for him and squeezed him close. Her tears spilled onto his coat. She couldn't conjure words. Peter was everything. Her reason for being.

Agatha was, too, but this was different. He'd made her a mom, his childhood passed in a blink, and then he was gone. Her heart was scarred.

When Peter stepped out of the way, he revealed a young woman. One of their kind, tall and graceful with a sweet face. "Mom, this is Seneca," he said. "My wife."

The words froze Mrs. Quatch. Peter was married, and she hadn't been there.

Seneca bounced on the balls of her feet. "Please pardon us for not calling. We were afraid you'd tell us not to come." Immediately, she clapped her hands over her lips. "I'm so sorry... I didn't mean..."

Mrs. Quatch reached for the girl's hands and squeezed them. "I understand. Do you want to come in?"

Peter's eyes moved from side to side. Mrs. Quatch could sense his fear. And Gordon must have, too, because he sidled up to Mrs. Quatch. She felt him bristle at the sight of Peter.

"Look who's here." Gordon smirked. Mrs. Quatch inched away from him, ready to put herself between her child and her husband if she had to.

Peter inclined his head. "Dad."

"What brings you here? Ah." Gordon's eyes landed on Seneca, who gave a tiny wave. "Your lovely lady?"

Peter drew Seneca closer. "My wife."

Mrs. Quatch sensed the pride in her son's voice.

Gordon raised his eyebrows. "Well, then. We'd be remiss if we didn't invite you in."

Mrs. Quatch stiffened as they went past. She hated her husband's expression—the way he assessed Seneca, considered her from top to toe.

THE REST of the family was surprised, but it was clear they took to Seneca, erasing some of the awkwardness. They asked her about her life, New Mexico, what it was like there. Things they would have asked Peter in another situation.

His wife kept eyeing him throughout dinner. Maybe hoping to get a read on his emotional state. Who knew. He pressed his lips together and remained stoic. He would get through this. They could spend the night in the woods before going home; it wasn't like they had to stay in the house. Seneca was just curious about his life before they met. That was all. When she rubbed her foot against his, her soft sole moving over his coarse fur, he felt a little better.

His mother brought out scads of dessert, which apparently his aunt had brought, judging by the way Minnie preened. Seneca ate and praised the pie, and he felt his insides fizzing.

Someone cleared their throat. Peter suddenly noticed his kid sister. Agatha's fur clanked with decorative beads, and her head was topped with a jaunty multicolored bow. She'd developed a smirk that sent Peter's resolve crumbling. He braced himself.

"Seneca, how do you feel about this new legislation in the pipeline? Cryptid rep, am I right?"

No one moved. Peter's heart sped up. Uncle Michael's mouth was set in a tight line. His mother looked like she might sink through the floor. Goddamn his sister.

"I'm for it," Seneca said smoothly. She brushed a swath of hair over one shoulder. "Peter and I advocate for cryptid rights. We deserve to be full members of society."

Peter didn't dare glance at his father.

Mrs. Quatch knew a bomb was about to go off.

She knew her husband. They'd grown up together, back before humans knew nothing of their existence. Gordon had liked it better that way, but more and more of their kind were decamping into human society. He was kind, a proper patriarch, but he was simple. He liked the old ways.

Why hadn't Peter explained this to the girl?

Mrs. Quatch could not lose her son again.

"We don't talk about politics here, dear." She laid a hand on Seneca's arm. "Maybe we could discuss the books we've recently read? Agatha and I both have library cards now."

Agatha rolled her eyes. "Yeah. Because the county finally voted to let us get them."

Mrs. Quatch seethed.

"That's wonderful," Seneca said. "We're waiting for that to happen on the reservation."

Mrs. Quatch dared to look around. Peter sat with his eyes facing forward. Gordon, though—he was watching Seneca curiously, like she was a specimen in a petri dish.

Seneca turned to her. "You have a lovely home. Can you point me to the restroom?"

"Thank you," Mrs. Quatch said. "It's right down the hall there. Across from the stairway."

Downstairs, the twins were clashing and clanging around. Minnie gritted her teeth and went after them, and Michael followed. The rest of the family—the family Mrs. Quatch had made—sat and stared at each other.

"You must love her a lot to make that long trip," Gordon said.

Peter nodded.

Agatha folded her arms. Mrs. Quatch could still remember the day she was born—all that beautiful black hair on her. It had never changed color, and Agatha looked like one of those goth human girls Mrs. Quatch saw in celebrity magazines. Her daughter even wore a little makeup—winged eyeliner and mascara. Agatha always made Mrs. Quatch feel dowdy. Mrs. Quatch had never been lovely.

Seneca, too, was a beautiful girl.

"Are you two going to acknowledge the mammoth in the room?" Agatha asked.

Mrs. Quatch bristled.

"I've forgiven Peter long ago," Gordon said dismissively. "It isn't my fault he left."

PETER WAS VERY STILL.

His father had forgiven him? He hadn't done anything wrong.

Seneca returned from the bathroom. Her palms smelled of lavender lotion. She shook her hair back and adjusted her chair. "Now what are we talking about?"

"Oh, nothing," said Peter's mom.

Agatha still had that cat-ate-the-canary look. "Oh, you know. Figuring out why Dad and Peter can't get their lives together."

"My life is fine," Peter's dad said. "He's responsible for his own decisions."

Peter wanted to go home. He wasn't a forest creature anymore. The desert suited him better. That dry air filled his lungs. Cratered hills, tall mountains, a hundred places to hide. Where he found his wife. Where he wasn't human, but he didn't have to be.

He looked over at his father. Gordon stared down at his empty plate, which was already crusting with crumbs. Peter had never gotten a true apology. He'd always wanted that. Peter was on the right side, after all.

Peter was quaking. He sat on his hands.

He realized he felt sorry for his father. Gordon always prided himself on "pulling himself up by his bootstraps." That he'd worked for this house, sacrificed himself for their family, and human-cryptid relationships didn't matter as long as they had what they needed. Peter knew his father had done that for them, and he appreciated it—that was true. But his father didn't even realize they were oppressed. He had drunk the Kool-Aid and shunned the very people who could have set him free.

Peter swallowed. They met each other's eyes, and he resisted the urge to look away. He saw himself in his father's face, in the way they stood, in the chestnut color of their hair.

The kids came flying up the steps, and Peter's focus broke.

His mother stood up. "You must stay the night."

"Oh no," Seneca said. "We weren't planning on it. We don't want to put you out."

Mrs. Quatch clucked. "You're family."

Peter squeezed Seneca's hand. "It's okay, Mom. We'll head out in the morning. Don't worry about us."

Mrs. Quatch didn't say she wanted him to stay because he was her baby. That it had been so long since he slept under her roof. And now

with his wife! She was so proud. "Will you come back in the morning before you leave?" she asked Seneca.

"We could do that." Seneca's jaw was set further back than most of her people's. She flashed bright white teeth. Mrs. Quatch wondered if the girl had work done to look more human.

Seneca elbowed Peter. "Say bye to your family. Don't you want hugs?"

She embraced Mrs. Quatch. The girl smelled like lavender. Mrs. Quatch could feel Seneca's heart beating against her own chest.

Peter did not seek out his sister or dad. He held his mother briefly. Just long enough for Mrs. Quatch to pull away feeling hollow.

Seneca pulled off her faux fur coat and piled it onto the seat beside her. "Do you think they suspected?"

"I wish you wouldn't do that," Peter said.

"What? You said I couldn't meet them unless I did this." She clicked the seat belt across her bare chest, then sighed and relaxed. "It was so hot."

"You're hot," Peter said. "You're distracting me."

She grinned and threw back her long hair.

They stayed out in the woods. Peter set up the tent, and they rolled inside. He loved the feel of his wife's smooth skin, her hands all over every part of his body. He found solace in the hollow of her neck, her clavicles, anything south. They stayed there until dawn.

In the morning, they packed their things. Peter knew they had promised his mother another visit. "C'mon," Seneca said." I bet she'll have coffee."

Peter nodded. His father drank gallons of it. "She does make good morning bread," he admitted.

Seneca's brow furrowed. "What's that?"

"It's like a bun. With cinnamon butter." He shook his head. "You'll have to try it."

She smiled. "Well, let's go."

He checked his phone as she pulled on the heavy suit, groaning.

There was a text, and Peter couldn't catch his breath for a second. Gordon Quatch was the sender. *I'm proud of you, son.*

Peter blinked. There was a pit in his stomach. He typed back. *Why?*

The three dots came up for only a second. His father wasn't hesitating to reply. *I see the way you look at her.*

He clutched the phone, but not too tight, lest he break it. *Do you love Mom like that?* he typed.

And Agatha. And you.

Peter didn't respond. Seneca was adjusting her Bigfoot hair. "How do I look?"

He sidled up to her and kissed her furry neck. "You're beautiful."

She sighed and drew a circle around her throat. "Do you think I still need this?"

He buried his face in the mountains of fake fur. She still smelled like herself under all of that.

"Yes," he said. "It's not time yet."

WHEEL OF FORTUNE

Another Saturday morning. I'm sitting on the couch with a cup of coffee, trying to will myself to move. The house needs a good cleaning, and I haven't touched the laundry in a week. "I'll just buy a new pack of socks," Frank says. "That'll get the kids through till you do it."

We don't have the money for such a frivolous purchase, but I keep that to myself. Frank knows it as well as I do. Our bathroom flooded last month after a pipe burst, and the insurance will only cover so much. Plus the four of us are sharing the downstairs bathroom. I'm sick of the sweat and stink of two boys and a husband. I miss my bathtub.

He's staring at his phone. I'm fixating on the rug, where there is a spot of brown from spilled coffee.

"Whoa." Frank stops scrolling. "Look at this."

Still blinking away sleep, I lean over.

It's a castle. A straight-on view: towering turrets with an open maw for a door. It is pitch black with a shimmering sheen. Painted brick? Whatever it is, I don't like it.

I sit back. "What is that?"

"An ad for a reality show. Contestants can win stuff if they stay in the castle for a week."

"Ah. That might be interesting to watch."

Not really. But if he wants to see it, I can sit on the couch with him and read.

We've all been in such a funk lately. Every day feels the same. My job used to be so interesting—I was an interior decorator and organization consultant. Which is so ironic considering the disaster of my house. But the inconsistency of my income meant I had to give it up for a nine-to-five as an administrative assistant for a tech company. Frank is in logistics and spends most of his time on calls. The boys do school and play video games.

"It's not for watching the show. They're looking for contestants." Frank turns his phone to show me an application form. "You in?"

I shudder. I already feel uncomfortable. "I don't know."

"It's not like we're gonna get picked." Frank untangles his long legs from under him and hunches over the screen.

"But if I don't want to do it, why bother applying?"

He looks up. "You said you didn't know."

I don't know. But if I keep saying that, he's going to think I mean that literally, when I mean I don't know why it creeps me out. So I shake my head. Sometimes it feels like I shouldn't even speak to Frank because he won't understand.

The sun is peeking through the windows, bathing us in light. I squint against the east-facing rays. Then I get up and stretch and head for the shower. I can listen to a podcast while I fold clothes. It'll help distract me from the monsters in that castle.

It's about three months later when we get the call.

Well, Frank gets the call, since he'd put in his phone number as the contact. We're in the kitchen on a weekday night. I'd been considering whether or not to make dinner or to let everyone fend for themselves. Anthony never leaves his room, and Robert is down the street at a friend's house.

"You'll never believe who that was." Frank takes two big steps and reaches for me, spins me around.

I squirm out of his grasp. "Who?"

"Stonecraft Media."

"Why would you be talking to a media company?" But I already know.

"*The Castle of Horrors.*" He's grinning. "The show. They want us."

My stomach feels heavy. "Are you sure? Don't they usually have you submit a video or something?"

"I did. Plus some pictures of you and the kids. I honestly thought there was no chance."

It's definitely a fend-for-yourself night. "Is there still time to say no?"

His face falls. "I'm sure there is, but..."

He did this without telling me. After I'd already said I wasn't sure. It feels like a betrayal. "Did you tell the kids?"

Frank waves a hand. "Oh yeah, of course. They're stoked. Do you know how much money we can win?"

I look down, trace my purple sock against the gray linoleum. We do need money. Anything we won would go a long way to replace the savings we've spent on the bathroom fiasco. We also need new windows. New gutters. New plumbing. New roof. New deck. The list goes on.

"Don't worry." He comes back over to me and puts an arm around my shoulders. I am reminded of our first dates, where I'd lean into him and he'd pull me close. He smells like sea salt and coconut. Like protection.

And I hate that, because I'm a strong woman and I can take care of myself. But maybe that's exactly why I can do this.

I straighten up. "Let's go win that money."

Robert sets up challenges for us. At nine, he's still a sneaky bastard, and when I hear ghostly moans in the night, I don't realize they're coming from his phone. I'm already panicking, shaking under my covers. It's past midnight when he comes in, giggling like a fiend. He turns off the sound effects and crawls into my bed. He still has such soft skin, hair that smells like lemons. It takes me a long time to fall asleep.

"Think about it, Maeve," Frank says to me in the morning. Robert is splayed between us and snoring. I've hung on to the edge of the bed all night. "All that stuff is going to be fake. It's not a real haunted castle. Yeah, I'm sure it'll be scary, but..."

It feels like spiders are crawling down my back, their tiny legs skittering on my skin. "Bring it on," I say, willing my voice not to shake.

Before we leave, I ask my friend Nyla to come over and help me straighten up. She loves cleaning other people's houses—not so much her own. "I'm not here for the aftermath," she always says. "I can go home feeling like I accomplished something."

We hand-wash all the dishes, scrub out the sink, vacuum all the floors. Pick up the boys' clothes, their Pokemon cards, their Lego. I am backed up on the laundry—it never ends—but we have enough clean clothes to last the week. My bag is packed and sitting by the door.

I'm sweeping the kitchen floor when I realize Nyla is looking at me askance. "What?" I ask her.

"You're scaring me," she says simply.

I stop my broom halfway through making a dirt pile. "How so?"

"This isn't you." She shakes her head, her ponytail of braids swinging. "You would never do this."

I smile. "You calling me a scaredy cat?"

"That's not it." She leans on the kitchen counter. "You seem disassociated. Almost like you don't think you'll be back."

I've known Nyla since kindergarten, when she sat behind me. Our little desks were in rows back then, not like the pods they have now in my kids' classrooms. At first she was mischievous, picking apart paper and flicking it into my hair. It took me a while, but I eventually fought back by pouring water on her seat. It's a wonder we ever became friends, but once we were, we were inseparable. She was my maid of honor and I was hers. I was married first, but we didn't like the word "matron."

Nyla is more in tune with me than Frank ever will be. And I'm picking up her vibes loud and clear.

"You're right," I say softly. "I don't feel good about this."

She crosses the kitchen and puts her hand on my shoulder, warm and comforting. I pull her in for a hug, and she holds on to me for a long time, squeezing as hard as she can. "You can still get out of it," she says against my cheek.

I want to. I really do. But my kids' excitement and Frank's determination bash against my mind. It wouldn't be fair to take that away from them. They want to win. And I do too—I just don't know how to do it.

"It's okay," I tell Nyla as I let her go. "I'll make it work."

ANTHONY STARTS WHINING AS SOON as we get in the car. "How am I supposed to last a week without my Switch?"

"None of us will have any electronics." In the front seat, where he can't see me, I roll my eyes so hard it hurts. "Besides, Dad and I didn't have any of this stuff when we were kids."

Frank shakes his head. I smooth my hand over his wild black hair, balding at the top. We had to make our own fun. Which was usually sneaking around, parking wherever we could find privacy. Sometimes we didn't even have privacy. I blush at the memory.

Robert is staring out the window, off in his own world. My youngest son lives in a world of his own making. He's mischievous, energetic, but he can also disappear for long stretches. A week without screens won't faze him. Unless we all go insane from the horror of this place.

We live several hours away from the castle, so it didn't make sense for us to be flown in like the other contestants. Frank goggled at the check we got for mileage, though. "If this is the kind of budget they have..." he marveled as he deposited it online.

"It's wear and tear on our car," I'd pointed out.

"Whatever. No matter what happens, we're a little richer."

Are we, though? The closer we get to the middle of nowhere, the more twisted my belly becomes. The thought of facing that door, that mouth to swallow us, fills me with dread. And I don't think things will get any better once we're inside.

We've been instructed to park around the back of the building. It's an ordinary dirt lot, nothing special. White vans fill the space, and show personnel mill about as they mess with cameras and micro-phones. For a moment, I relax. This is nothing but television trickery. There are no actual ghosts in this castle.

Except I'm not sure if it's ghosts I'm afraid of.

We pile out of the car. Frank points and whispers, "That's the execu-tive producer. Winnie Barlow. And the host is Jack Sunshine. You remember him from *The Star of the Show*?"

"Of course not. I don't watch reality television."

"Neither do I. But I don't live under a rock." He edges closer to me. "The winner got to star in a Broadway show."

"The title suggests that, yes." I peer across the lot, trying to get a glimpse of this oh-so-famous fellow. "But is Sunshine his actual last name?"

Frank shrugs. "Probably not. But he sure looks like a Sunshine, doesn't he?"

It's a nice fall day, probably 55 degrees, and the trees are turning to brilliant yellows and reds. We're surrounded by them, a gorgeous palette of color. I take a long breath in and glance back to the kids. Robert seems antsy, while Anthony is sulking. I really don't love having a teenager.

Maybe I'm only scared because this is something unknown—some-thing new. It could be all kinds of corny stuff, hyped up for TV, each of us cast as a character for viewers to love or hate. I'll probably be the hated one. That's not even fiction.

The producer catches sight of us and heads our way. She has cherry red hair and wire-rimmed glasses. Her camel coat is topped off with a massive plaid scarf. She must be from the West Coast.

Winnie shakes our hands with the enthusiasm of youth. She can't be older than 25. "I'm so glad you're here! The locals!" She sweeps her arm toward the massive stone building behind us. "Have you visited before?"

"The town, yes." I nod. "Not... this place."

"It's unique, that's for sure. Our assistants scoured the country for the best location. I'm so excited for this show to come out." Winnie bounces on her brown Doc Martens. "It's my first big project. And we have Jack!"

I check back on the kids again. They're both still mute. Anthony is kicking the dirt.

"Will we meet him? I mean, he'll be filming with us, right?" Frank sounds a little too eager. I hadn't realized he was this starstruck.

Winnie nods. "At dinner. Right now we want to get some footage of your reaction to the castle entrance."

An icy finger traces its way down my spine.

Winnie gestures to a gaggle of people standing in a grassy area up by the trees. "Those are your roommates for the week. Or as long as you make it before you leave."

"Not contestants, though, right?" Frank asks.

"You're contestants, but not competitors. You get to keep anything you win throughout the week. The longer you stay, the better the prizes. Highest prize total at the end gets to the bonus round... if any of you are still alive."

Another shiver, this time wrapping around my hips.

"So it's like *Wheel of Fortune*? The game show?" Frank continues, oblivious.

Winnie grins. "Even better."

We climb the hill and join our fellow contestants, who are chatting. Getting to know each other. There are a few teenagers and kids around Anthony and Robert's ages, and I'm relieved when they strike up a conversation. I was afraid I'd have to entertain my children here, but my kids are good about making fast friends. Frank starts talking to an affable-looking man with a dress shirt and a small beer belly. I keep quiet. I'll blend into the background so no one has a chance to hate me.

It isn't long until Winnie approaches us, clapping. "Okay, everyone's here! It's time!"

A murmur goes through the group. I clutch Frank's hand. We move like an undulating mass, inching around the front of the building.

It's as bad as I thought. That mouth of the dragon, sharp teeth on all sides, that glimmering black brick. Green smoke blooms out from inside, heading toward us like an ethereal chain.

Gasps and screams fly into the air.

The smoke continues, transforming from mist to a tangible thing. A rope wrapping from the dragon's mouth to our waists, binding us together. *This must be fake,* I tell myself even as the green lash takes hold.

Then we are moving, our feet in step, our hands and waists held tight. Anthony breathes heavily into my ear. I want to grab his hands, to pull him closer to me, but both of us are manacled so tightly. There is crying from a child somewhere—Robert? It doesn't sound like him.

Our feet stumble through the sharp crags below us. Someone falls with a scream. I crane my neck, but someone else is screaming, "Don't look! We have to keep moving!"

Then, as quickly as we were tied, we are released.

Everyone pitches forward. We cluster into our families. My heart is hammering, but as Anthony and Robert surround me, I realize they're not at all scared. They're grinning, as is Frank. The family with the screaming little girl is being ushered away.

"That was SO cool," Robert marvels as he dances around my legs. His head still only comes up to my hips.

"If the rest of this is the same, I won't even need my Switch," Anthony says.

"We've got this. We're gonna make it." Frank grabs my clammy hand. "Hey. Maeve. You okay?"

I squeeze the tears out of my eyes. "Yeah. Yeah, I'm okay."

A PRODUCTION ASSISTANT jumps in to take our bags. There's no time to visit our rooms before dinner. Everything is set up, the cameras poised to film. We are miked and ready.

Each family is assigned a producer. Ours is a mild-mannered woman named Barbara. She sets us up at our table, makes sure we're in the right line of sight. "I'll let you know when to chime in," she says. "All the groups should get screen time. Now, since you're not competing, we won't pit you against each other. The villain on this show is the castle."

"Great," I mumble.

We are seated with an older middle-aged couple, Jay and Emil, on one side. On the other is the McMillan family: Lilly, Ryan, and their children, Kaydence and Ralph (pronounced "Rafe," because of course it is). Lilly is one of those moms who looks put together on the surface but is probably a hot mess inside. Her hair is long, dark, and blown out, her body sculpted like working out is her job. Ryan is a basic white guy in a polo and slacks. The kids are about the same ages as Anthony and Robert, and they'd already met outside. It isn't long until they're deep in conversation about their latest favorite Roblox games.

I can barely eat the salad they bring to us, let alone the chicken pasta dish entree. No one else seems bothered. I slip my extra food to the boys.

"So what made you want to come here?" Emil asks me.

Emil is the more talkative of that pair. He's also more casual, wearing a sweater and jeans, while Jay is buttoned up into a collared shirt and suit jacket. No tie, though. They're both handsome, the kind of men who get more attractive as they age. Jay's so white he's nearly transparent, while Emil's skin is a warm olive.

I turn to Frank. *We need the money* isn't the greatest look.

"For the adventure," my husband says, puffing up his chest. "Maeve and I, we've been doing the same things for years. Go to work, come home, watch TV, go to bed. The boys are growing. Soon they won't want anything to do with us. So now's the time."

Emil nods. "We're here for that too, kind of. Well, we don't have kids, but it's easy to get stuck in a rut."

I peek at Jay, wondering if he feels the same, and note his twisted expression. Something is off.

"You okay, man?" Ryan, seated next to Jay, pats the other man on the back.

Jay's already-pale face is turning green. He gets up and runs, tearing off his microphone as he careens toward a trash can. The cameras swivel to follow him. This is great television.

Does Emil have regrets? He keeps his eyes closed, doesn't go after his husband.

When Jay finally returns, he's carrying a can of ginger ale. He pushes his plates away. "I hope no one else gets sick," he says in a small voice.

WE'RE GIVEN a reprieve from filming so we can get our things to the room and freshen up. Our quarters are no-nonsense but comfortable. We have a window with a view of the parking lot. Our little car seems so far away.

There's another gathering before bedtime. When we return to the main hall of the castle, the eating tables have been cleared away. There's a long, imposing table surrounded by ornate chairs with plush purple upholstery. Barbara indicates our seats. Now we're beside a young-ish childfree couple. The woman has purple hair and cat-eye liner. The man wears glasses and has a shock of brown hair. He resembles Frank in a way.

Lately, I've been flashing back to our early days. How much we loved each other, how we were each other's best friends. How we couldn't keep our hands off each other. This couple—they introduce themselves as Bea and Lance—they are in that romantic phase. Their hands are crushed together, their thighs touching.

I reach under the table and take Frank's hand. He jumps at the unexpected touch but then holds tight.

Jack Sunshine's makeup is caked on, his skin approaching an orange hue. He's thin, his hair in a quiff, and he wears a slim-cut suit. Very hipster. He steps in front of us and spreads his hands wide. "My brave contestants! Welcome!"

There is a smattering of applause.

"Tonight, you will encounter your first evening in this place." The host turns in a circle, arms still outstretched. "You've signed up for a memorable experience. Even if you don't make it through the first night, your choice shows your mettle and tenacity. I've stayed here, and I can confirm that It. Is. Terrifying."

My leg starts to jiggle. Frank places his palm over my knee. Beside him, the kids are squirming.

"Before I let you go, we have an important task. Some of you will not survive this night, but those who do will take home whatever prizes you earn throughout the week."

Will not survive?

"Our first game is simple." He moves away to reveal a giant dragon head not unlike the front door of the castle. But instead of black, it's a shimmering green, with a red fiery mouth and glittering yellow eyes. It stares me down as if I'm the only one in the room.

"Everyone needs to put their hand inside the dragon's mouth. Whatever paper slip you pull out will be your cash prize." Jack sweeps his hand down and steps away. "My friends up front, you're on."

The contestants form a line. One would think that sticking a hand down a dragon's throat would incite some trepidation. But everyone is gleeful as they pull out their prize money. Some only get $1 or $5. Others uncover $5000 or even $10,000. I hear the victors squealing in delight.

My heart is hammering as I step forward. I close my eyes before plunging my hand into the maw.

A tentacle whips up from some dark place and snags my wrist. I take a sharp breath and struggle to let go. I allow myself a quick glance up to see that no one notices my predicament. Meanwhile, the squishy tentacle draws my arm deeper.

I shriek, and it stops all motion in the room.

"You okay?" Jack Sunshine steps over. I can smell the newness of his shirt, the gel holding up his hair.

The tentacle lets go. I blink, and the prize paper is under my fingers. I pull it out, and Jack plucks it from my hand.

"Well done, Maeve!" We are all wearing name tags. "Three thousand!"

My kids whoop and cheer. The rest of them pull hundreds, leaving us at $3300.

"Remember, everyone—your daily totals add up. But you won't collect anything until you reach the end of the week." Jack claps his hands. "Now it's time for bed!"

~

I'm the only one awake.

The room is quiet. The overhead fan creates a soft white noise. Frank is snoring away, and I can hear the kids breathing across the room in their bed.

I still feel the hold of the tentacle around my wrist, the chains around my waist. The realization dawns on me that I won't sleep this entire week. If we make it through. But so far no one in my family has been troubled. There must be something wrong with me. To be honest, that's not a new feeling.

I lean back against the headboard. The quiet is threatening my sanity too. I could listen to an audiobook or a podcast on my phone, but then I'd miss any sounds from outside. I have to be vigilant.

"It's all fake anyway," Frank had said before we went to bed. "They're the ones making stuff scary. There's no need to be upset. We'll sleep our way through the week and take home tons of money."

Had they not experienced everything I did when we were being pulled inside? No tentacles encircled their wrists and wouldn't let go?

As the night wears on, I remember when the boys were little, when I had to nurse them or comfort them, when they needed diaper changes, when they wet the bed. This time of night is both magical and terrible. There's a deep peace when no one is awake, yet the threats of the dark remain.

I'm almost about to doze off when I hear it.

A faint scratching. A soft whine. As if a small animal is crawling in the walls.

Adrenaline pops in my veins. *Could be nothing,* I tell myself.

Could be anything.

The temperature in the room plummets. I am suddenly freezing, and I snatch up the blanket around me, but it does little good. The scratching continues, louder now, and the whine turns into a full-fledged tornado siren.

I smash my hands against my ears as I struggle to stay wrapped in the comforter. Goosebumps prickle along my arms. No one wakes. I am the only one to see the frost that begins inching up the windows. As the small trails begin sticking together, the mass moves as one, continuing until it covers the entire pane.

I picture the window shattering, the glass spilling onto my kids' skin, cutting them up.

I get up and peer out the window. Almost all the panes are closing with ice, but I can see out the last one.

And then I scream. Again.

Our outdoor view is gone. No parking lot, no trees—nothing of the normal world. Everything outside is green and gray. If I squint, I can see more structures like this one in the background. Bats flutter in the cloud-choked air.

Huge creatures walk toward us. They're black from head to toe, wearing equally huge capes with tattered hoods. Besides those, they're only clothed in shadow.

My senses prick, and my shivering increases. I have no doubt they have caused all this. The whine, the cold, the anger that bubbles inside me. No one is backing me up. I am completely alone.

I'm about to wake up my family when one of the creatures speaks to me.

"Maeve of Earth," it booms inside my head. I can hear that whine and scratch beneath each word. "You have provided us with an opportunity. We salute you."

"Where have you come from?" I whisper.

"You received us this morning. When you drew the slips from the dragon's mouth."

"But I thought..."

"Each of you faces a different fight." Soon the creatures were fully within my sight and closing in on the windows. "We are prepared for all of you."

I shake my head. "No. You can't do this."

One of the creatures laughs, a sickening sound that turns my stomach. "We can do anything we want."

The next thing I see is a body being lifted to the air. No pulleys or surfaces. Just a body, dangling there. I can't see if the person is alive or dead, and I hope for God's sake that they have passed on.

Another creature asks me, "Have you ever seen a surgery before?"

"Of course I have," I say defensively.

"Good. Then this will hurt us more than it hurts you."

The body splits apart. Flesh and blood spits in every direction. Gore and intestines dangle from the corpse.

I wail and turn away. I couldn't see if the person was from the show, but they were most definitely human. Long, dark hair was the only feature I could capture. That person is nameless now.

Tears squeeze out and run down my cheeks. I am done. We leave here tomorrow.

When everyone wakes up, I'm packing our things.

"That wasn't scary at all," Frank says as he yawns and stretches. "How about you, boys?"

Robert shrugs. "Not scared."

Anthony doesn't seem completely sure, but then again, I took all his video games away. He's probably going through withdrawal. "Mom, you were up all night."

I stop mid-fold. "How did you know?"

"Woke up and saw you staring out the window."

I yawn, proving his point. "You're right. I saw strange things. Things that make me want to leave."

Anthony gets up. He's still in his frog pajamas, the ones I love because they're so irreverent and so Anthony. Each frog proclaims *It's*

Wednesday, my dudes. Even though it is decidedly not Wednesday. It's Monday, and we have to make it to Friday.

Anthony wraps his arms around me. "It's gonna be okay, Mom."

"I don't know." I look around briskly. "Can I leave the game if you three stay?"

Frank's lips tighten into a line. "No. Family groups must stay together. It's in the contract."+

It's good to know he actually read the contract. But I don't know if I can do this again.

Breakfast is downstairs in the main hall. The caterers are serving grilled sausage and omelets. I don't take anything except a strong cup of coffee.

"Okay, people!" Jack Sunshine yells. "Time to find out who made it."

The group is smaller than it was last night, but I can't tell who exactly is gone. The cameras crowd around us, also searching.

Jack tells us to stand when he calls our names. I'm on shaky legs, but I heave myself up. He doesn't call the McMillans, and indeed, their chairs are empty. So at least one group is down. Robert and Anthony sulk, their newfound friends already gone.

"Eight sets of contestants left," Jack announces. "That's two families out of the game. Congratulations to all of you who made it through the night unscathed!"

Everyone claps, including the producers and equipment operators.

My breath hangs in my chest. *Lilly McMillan with her long dark hair.* Was she the person I saw destroyed last night?

WE ARE outside for the day's challenges. The sky is azure blue, wispy clouds floating aimlessly above us. It's a bit chilly, but the temperature doesn't seem to bother the other players.

Winnie Barlow steps in front of us, framed by orange and red foliage from the trees behind her. She is annoyingly cute in a sweater dress, tights, and knee-high brown boots. I glance at Frank as he eyes her.

"Hi everyone!" She flashes that high-wattage smile. "As you can see, I'm not Jack. But I'll be subbing in for him this morning. He needs a break."

I need a break. I'm an inch away from curling up on the grass for a nap.

"This will be our shooting competition. Before you get too scared, we're not using guns." Winnie steps to the side and brandishes a bow and arrow. "Each team will get six chances to hit the targets on those wheels right there."

Down the field from her are eight spinning wheels, black lines dividing them into six canvas wedges. Dollar amounts and images are printed on them.

"We're in a castle, so it only makes sense to practice our marksmanship." She walks over to us and hands Frank the archery set she's holding. I cringe as his gaze lingers. "You decide which of your teammates will be competing. You can each shoot, or you can choose one or two of your best players."

I wipe my hands on my jeans and turn to my family. "Well, I'm out."

Anthony jumps beside me. "You can do it, Mom! Believe in yourself!"

"I believe that if you want to win, you should not let me shoot." I pat Anthony on the back. "Aren't you missing your games? You'd be good at this."

My older son puffs up his chest. "You know, I don't miss them that much. This is better."

Frank and I exchange a glance. Robert is also jumping, his shorter stature requiring him to hop higher.

I hear Frank's voice in my head, part of our couple telepathy. *We can't leave now. Not when the kids aren't dying without screen time.*

Tears prick my tired eyes. "Honestly, boys, I'm tapped out. I'll watch."

I stand back, and Anthony takes the bow. Each kid tries one shot, and then Frank goes. Their arrows fly across the field, falling into the grass wide of the wheels. Some hoots and hollers fill the air with victory, but after Anthony sends the fourth one almost into the woods, I'm pretty sure we're not getting any rewards from this challenge.

My chest grows cold. A thread of ice fills my mouth and snakes down into my stomach. I half expect my body to split open, like Lilly's did last night. I fall to the ground, on my knees, and vomit out a long trail of green mist.

The mist travels from my body and takes hold of the bow as Robert aims it. I'm on the hard ground, gasping, watching as Robert's arrow shoots straight and true right into the wedge with a car icon printed on it.

No one notices that I've fallen. They've all surrounded the boys as they whoop and celebrate. We've won a car, and there is still one more arrow left. Robert hands the bow to Anthony, and that mist reappears. The arrow hits another car wedge, and everyone is jumping and screaming while I heave against the ground.

"Mom, can you believe it? It's like a dream!" Robert clutches my arm and shakes me. "Two cars! We won two cars!"

Night is coming again. The closer it gets, the harder my heart hammers. I have this *thing* inside me now, and who will it claim next?

My kids have not been able to settle down all evening. They might have if Jack Sunshine hadn't come over to congratulate us personally. The excitement bubbled up again, and now they can't stop bouncing.

I'm sitting in front of the second-floor fireplace with Emil. Jay has gone to bed, citing a stomachache. The fire is cozy, but every few seconds I see a flick of green amid the orange-yellow blaze. I blink hard, forcing myself awake.

Emil sits on the armchair across from the one I'm in. He's casual, legs crossed, glass of white wine in hand. "So how did your first night go?" he asks me.

"Not great, to be honest." I put my head down, stare at the red carpet decorated with gold fleur-de-lis. "It was fucking scary."

Emil snorts. "They're going to kick you out for language like that."

"They can always bleep it out." I look up, searching for the cameras they've hidden in the walls and ceiling. "Hear that? Bleep it out."

He chuckles and takes a sip of his wine. "What was scary about it?"

I'm scared to admit it. Scared to describe the horrors that have been filling me since the moment we came in here. It seems that no one else is as tortured as I am.

I finally settle on a compromise. "I can't describe it," I say.

Emil lowers his voice. "Jay has said the same. Did you see him at the challenge?"

I can barely recall. I was too busy vomiting out the entire contents of my haunted stomach.

"He was sick," Emil goes on without waiting for me to speak. "He sat on the ground the whole time. I shot all six arrows."

"Did you win anything?" I'd been practically catatonic by the time Winnie announced prizes.

"A good forty thousand," he says with another triumphant sip of wine. "That money will change our lives."

Wasn't that what Frank had said? Yet none of them seem fazed at all. The only person getting her life changed is me.

"I'm glad for you," I tell him, meaning it. I can only hope Jay isn't suffering like I am.

～

TONIGHT, they're waiting for me.

Once everyone is asleep, they float into the room. A long shadowy finger curls in the air, beckoning me back. I don't have a choice but to follow.

The hallway is quiet. I trail the creatures, stepping carefully onto the carpet. It squishes between my toes, covered in a sticky substance. *Blood*, I think at first, but when I look down I see that my socks are stained by a thick green slime.

And then the figures are gone. I'm standing alone in the hallway, shivering, my feet blocks of ice.

I turn and creep in the opposite direction, heading toward our room. *Why would they do this? I wonder. What's their endgame? Just to lure me in and take me back out again?*

I keep moving, as softly as I can, until I reach the door.

Once I'm inside, all I see is hellfire.

Huge creatures, made of pink brain-like tissue, hover in the air above a ground made of rock and bone. The sky is green, lit by a neon that emerges from the cracks between the rocks. The creatures have long tentacles, and I hear screams as they smack bodies in the air. The tentacles create an eerie flash of lightning each time they hit.

I stand motionless.

The floating bodies are Nyla and Jay.

They're moaning. Nyla throws her head back. One tentacle is wrapped around her neck, the others punishing her torso and legs. Her hair dangles down, moving back and forth each time the creature strikes her. Jay clutches his stomach, trying to push away the tentacle that's wrapping his abdomen. Every few moments, he tries to vomit, but nothing comes out.

I drop to my knees and cover my face. "Stop it! Stop it!"

"Maeve of Earth." The same booming voice echoes through the hellscape. "You have seized your opportunity."

I can't breathe, let alone speak. Even with my face covered, I can still hear them. The green light still flashes behind my palms.

"For triumph, there must be a sacrifice."

One tentacle rakes down Jay's body. He ekes out one final scream, and then the creature drops him. He lies motionless on the cracked ground.

I scream. "You can't do this to me. I don't want to be here. I don't want to trade their lives for luck."

"What you want is irrelevant."

The mind flayers—I suddenly know what they are, unbidden— double up on Nyla. Her shrieks pierce the insides of my ears.

"You will not touch her!" I cry as I get up. I plant my gross, slimy feet on the ground and take a deep breath, then suck all the energy around me into my body and push it out.

The same green mist pours from my lips and wraps itself around Nyla. It pulls her back to me, and she lies panting on the ground.

She reaches up to cup my cheek. "Thank you."

"You aren't supposed to be here," I weep as I hold her close. "You told me not to be scared."

Her voice is raspy. "I'll say the same thing now."

"Even after all that?"

Nyla is fading. "Even after all that."

And then she disappears into dust.

IN THE MORNING, my socks are dry.

I don't even wait for my family to get up. I rush downstairs, where they're setting up for breakfast. Jack Sunshine is sitting in a corner getting his makeup done. Winnie is on the phone, pacing back and forth on the stone tile by the cavernous front door.

"I need my phone." I rush up to her, breathless. "Please. It's an emergency."

Winnie, still on her phone, frowns at me. "Hold on a sec," she says to her caller, then turns to me. "How would you know if there is an emergency if you don't have your phone?"

I want to shake her. "What do you know about this place? Did you do any research before bringing us here?"

Her lip twists, and she waves me off. "I can't have this conversation now."

"Didn't you say we could leave anytime we want?"

She turns her back to me.

"Winnie." My words are sharp-edged, loud. I want to draw attention to myself. I want people to know that this house isn't haunted. There are no ghosts here. These are evil creatures, creatures that will worm their way inside you, cause you to go insane. "I need my phone. Now."

She turns, the phone now in her hand, the person on the other end squawking. "I need you to shut up and get back to the floor."

I'm about to go apeshit on her when I see my family coming

down the stairs. Frank is cheerful, and both boys are bright-eyed. They look rested and happy. Something turns in my stomach, a hard cramp.

Fine. I'll cede to her this time. But I am going to find out what happened to Nyla. I just have to go about it a different way.

Jack Sunshine calls the names of the people who have made it through the night. As expected, more families have disappeared. But I'm most shocked that Emil is there while Jay is not.

Once we've disbanded for the morning, I sidle up to Emil. My body is still amped from worry for Nyla, but after seeing Jay tortured last night, I'm terrified for him too. "Where's Jay?" I whisper. "I thought we weren't allowed to split up."

Emil turns to me. His once olive-colored skin is now deathly pale. He looks like he's been through a war. While everyone else goes off to prepare for the next challenge, he slumps into a seat.

"What happened?" I whisper, sinking into the chair beside him.

"He's gone." Emil's voice is hoarse. I wait for him to say more, but nothing comes.

"What do you mean? Where did he go?"

Emil leans forward and pitches his head into his hands. He starts rubbing his hair, faster and faster until I think it's going to catch fire. Then he starts pulling at the hair, at his ears. When he finally sits up, he's driving his nails into his jeans while he rocks in place like a little boy.

"Emil." I place my hand on his shoulder, but he violently shrugs me off. I jam my hand under my butt and take my tone down a notch. "Emil, talk to me. Last night I saw Jay get hurt. And one of my friends was there. Did you see that? Did you see the green fire?"

He nods, still rocking.

"Why haven't they let you go home?"

"Don't... want..." His throat is so dry. I jump to my feet and fetch him a glass of water. He starts to relax enough for me to press the glass into his hands. After taking a small sip, he speaks again. "I need to get him back."

"We can do it. I'll go with you tonight. Can you make it?"

He can't speak because Winnie comes stomping over, her perfectly coiffed hair flying, a vengeful angel in riding boots. "Mr. Sanders, I asked you to leave."

Emil cuts his eyes up to her and slowly rises to his feet. I follow.

He's probably five-ten, but she's a pixie, and he stares her down. "I'm not leaving without my husband."

Winnie rolls her eyes. "Your husband is fine. After he told us he wanted to leave, we took him offsite. Just come with me and I'll reunite the two of you."

"No." His voice is still scratchy, but it's gaining power. "I saw what you did to him last night."

The producer takes a step back. "I don't know what you're talking about."

"The green fire? The hellscape?" Emil moves closer, close enough to spit in her face if he wanted to. "The demons who refused to spare him?"

She scoffs. "Enough with these dramatics."

Emil roars and charges the girl, picks her up with muscles I didn't know he had. He presses her against the wall, hands around her neck, squeezing.

I'm frozen in place.

A team of workers rushes over and pries Emil off Winnie. He bares his teeth at her as they hold him back. Another producer ushers Winnie away, murmuring about getting her to the set medic. "We need police here right away," a production tech growls into a walkie-talkie.

I have no choice but to pretend I was never even there. I flee the scene, my footsteps pattering wildly on the cobblestones.

WITHIN THE HOUR, the contestants reconvene in the main hall. There is no sign of either Emil or Winnie. Jack Sunshine, looking decidedly less sunshiny, faces us, flanked by a junior producer.

Jack is wringing his hands in front of him. His makeup is melting as he sweats, and his eyes are hollowed out with dark. "I'm so sorry to all of you," he says. "But we have to cancel the show."

The crowd immediately starts chattering, yelling. Frank, beside me, tenses up, while the kids are moaning and wailing. "No," Anthony says in a long whine. "We won all that stuff!"

"Now we aren't even going to be on TV," Robert says mournfully.

Frank reaches for my hand, and I turn toward him. He's crying. I only remember seeing him cry when the boys were born. Not even on our wedding day.

I am both relieved and scared. I'll be able to go home and check on Nyla. What I saw must have been a hallucination. But where is Jay, and where have they taken Emil? And the McMillans?

"All of you will be compensated for your efforts here," Jack says. "A producer will be with you to settle up, and then you can leave."

"Well, at least I'll get my Switch back," Anthony grumbles. "Do me and Robert get a cut of the money?"

"I don't know, kid." Frank's face is ashen. "You two go up and start packing, okay? I need to talk to your mom."

I'm so tired that everything in front of me is spinning. Frank leads me to one of the couches in the sitting area near the fireplace. The other families and couples are roaming restlessly as they wait for their turns with the producers. Frank's knee touches mine, and I'm already worrying about what he's going to say. Along with the hundred other things I'm petrified about.

"I thought for sure we were going to make it through this." His presence is comforting, his warmth and his scent, but I can feel a tension between us. "We really need that money."

"We'll be okay without it." I put my palm over his knee. "Honestly, babe, we've got more important things to worry about."

"You don't understand." Frank squeezes my hand, and I'm suddenly reminded of Emil and his childlike rocking. "I haven't been completely honest with you."

Dread fills my body, as icy as the frost the demons cursed me with.

"You know how I've been staying up late?"

I roll my eyes. "Yeah, because you're so obsessed with those games."

"I've been playing online poker."

I am not hearing this.

"We've lost some money," Frank continues.

"We've lost money?" I stare at him incredulously. "You mean you lost money. How much?"

He swallows. "About ten grand."

"Jesus!" I shriek, causing other competitors to turn their heads. The woman with the purple hair tosses me a particularly judgy sneer.

I jerk my hand out from under my husband's. "Frank! How could you do this?"

"I don't know. I just... it was a lark, and it became more than that."

"An addiction." I shake my head. I'm clutching the couch's hard metal arm now. "And you thought doing something like this would make it better?"

"I wanted to make it go away. And hopefully have some left over to treat you to something you wanted."

I can't respond. I'm so exhausted. "Frank, I have to figure this out. We can talk about this later."

His beetle brows raise up. "You're not mad?"

"I'm not saying that. It's just... there are a lot of other issues." I blink, trying to keep the room in focus. The fireplace in front of us is dead, the charred remains of logs covering the metal grille inside. "What happened at night that was supposed to scare you?"

Frank shrugs. "There were some thumps and bumps. Some noises. I figured the show people were doing it. And the boys didn't even wake up. Why?"

"That's not..." I realize I can't explain it to Frank. It isn't that he can't know—it's just that he won't understand. No one except Emil has seen what I saw. I don't even think Winnie knows. She's been a fickle bitch this morning, but she doesn't look haunted. Not like Emil and I are.

I start again. "Things have been really strange here."

He doesn't look mad, just confused, his forehead furrowing.

But then the producer comes over to him with a stack of papers and a pen, and he turns to them, and I slip quietly away.

❦

THEY GIVE us our phones back, and I immediately call Nyla as I stand beside the empty fireplace.

She answers. "What's so important that you had to call?"

"Nothing, I..." *She sounds okay. Please let her be okay.* "I was worried about you."

"Why? I should be more worried about you. What's going on at that crazy house?"

She has no idea. I am relieved at the warm tone of her voice in my ear, until I wonder... is this an illusion too? Is one of these demons play-acting as her to make me think she's alive?

"Hey, can you answer me something?" My wrists are tight as I clutch the phone. "Where did we meet?"

"Huh?"

"Where did we meet?"

"They take your memory or something?"

I sink onto the couch. Frank and the kids have already gone upstairs to pack. We're leaving here. I can go back and check on her when we get home, but what will I find? An evil representation of my best friend?

"Please just tell me. I need to know."

Nyla sighs. "Kindergarten. That help?"

"Can you be more specific?"

"You sat in front of me and I used to drop paper on your head." She harrumphs. "I thought you were a dumb kid until we started hanging out."

"Hey! You've never told me that before!" My hand goes a little slack on the edge of the phone. This might be okay. We're getting somewhere.

"You said you wanted more specifics." She laughs. "So you're coming home?"

"Yeah. But hey, I need to ask you something else. Has anything weird been happening around you while I've been here?"

Nyla hums. It sounds like she's on her lunch break, sitting outside the Subway she likes, cars going past as she enjoys her sandwich. I like picturing her there, somewhere safe, somewhere she wants to be.

"The fucked-up dream I had last night," she says with no preamble. "Really fucking creepy, Maeve. There was all this green light and creepy monsters trying to eat me."

THE SUN IS FADING as we step into the parking lot. The crew is dismantling the set, putting away their gear. Jack Sunshine has been whisked away. It's hard to believe any television show—or the promise of one—happened here.

I'm about to get in the car. The kids have already unearthed their Switches and are bent over them. Frank is already in the driver's seat. He's pleased with the five thousand we received for being on the show. Only five thousand to go to pay off that debt. It's a start.

But that's a problem for later. I consider the castle, looming up in front of me. I have unfinished business there. We're driving hours back to our home, and I'm going to leave those demons here to torture and kill more people? Who's the caretaker of this place, anyway? Did Winnie sign a contract with blood?

"Go on without me," I say to Frank.

"What?" He cranes his neck at an awkward angle to see me. "Why?"

"Or at least go stay in town. I need another night here."

"Mom!" Anthony cries. "Let's just go. I want to get back to normal life."

Robert is so ensconced in his game that he doesn't add his two cents.

I don't want to go back to our "normal" life. Where my actions don't matter and nothing ever changes. I need to rescue the people who have gone missing. Nyla must have been too far away for them to grasp—a vision to scare me—but Jay and Lilly McMillan were swallowed by these entities. Maybe even the entire McMillan family. And maybe Emil too.

"I've seen some things," I say plainly. "Things that were never revealed to you. The true haunting in this castle."

"Don't be cryptic." Frank gets out of the car and slams the door, walks around to where I'm standing. "What's the deal? We need to get home."

I walk through the details of what I'd experienced the last two nights. Frank is skeptical at first, but his skin grows paler as I talk.

"I need to figure out if I can save them," I tell him finally. "They're here somewhere."

Frank blows out a long breath and runs a hand through his hair. I get it. He thinks I'm insane. That my sleep deprivation has pulled all the logic out of me. But I have no choice. One more night to fight them. One more night to beat these things.

"Come on, kids," he says, opening the backseat doors. "Back inside."

THE CASTLE IS EERILY EMPTY. There is no front desk. No craft services or crew. We might be the only ones here. Without ambient sound to dampen any noise, our footsteps echo throughout the main hall.

We crowd back into the room we've just left. By now it is mid-afternoon, and we are all dragging. The three of them are immediately absorbed in their screens and are chomping on the snacks we brought for the car—Combos, Chex Mix, chips.

I can't think. I'm alone in my own head. But I can't sleep. Not until I can ensure everyone's safety.

Even mine.

We don't leave the room all evening. It isn't long before the three of them pass out. I've promised them a big breakfast in the morning to atone for this wild mission.

The noises begin once the sun has set. Eerie clanking, moaning. Like what Frank said he and the boys could hear. But this time they sleep through all of it. And the crew isn't here to create the illusion. My time is near.

I don't wait. I get up and charge into the hall.

"Where are they, you bastards?" I yell. "Come on. You said I provided you an opportunity. Now I have a proposal. Give them back and I'll never bother you again."

A wicked laugh echoes throughout the corridor.

I don't think. I chase it.

I'm running now, wending my way through the halls. The laugh is escalating, bouncing against the black stone. But I'm not getting closer to it. The sound wafts away, taunting me.

I slow down when I realize I'm outside our door again. I've been running in a circle. I'm nowhere close to these assholes.

"Please," I beg. "Let me help them. I'll leave you alone."

"You will not leave us alone." The booming voice finally speaks, wrapping me in a cold chain. "We are here because you called us."

"I did not!" I spit. "This is a stupid game. They called it off. I need to go home now."

"You will not go home."

One of the creatures materializes in the air before me. This one wears a white hood that obscures its face. When I get closer, I see that its phantom entrails spin out from its false body.

Its bony finger points at me. "You will never leave."

My stomach churns. My legs go weak, then start burning with unholy acid. I collapse to the ground, and an unearthly force bends me toward them as if in worship. They have full control of me. I am done.

Tomorrow, they'll go. I won't keep my family here. I'll insist that I have to stay and I won't come back. Before long, they'll forget I exist. I'll be a distant memory.

Screams poke inside my ears, all the way to the tender insides that abut my brain.

The creature wraps its misty tendrils around me, and I'm airborne. It holds me back like the others were held, in the perfect position to be flayed alive. The green-white knife is in the air as if the creature has never picked it up. I brace myself for the inevitable.

My family's door flies open, and Frank and the boys burst outside. Anthony brandishes the bow he won at the game. Robert and Frank growl and rush the creature, though they grasp at nothing as its body starts fading. Anthony aims and puts his arrows through the creature's bloody middle. They fall to the floor on the other side of it. The creature stares blankly at them.

"You think such petty attacks can assuage us?" The creature spits out a bolt of green light, and it wraps around my family.

I let go of my tension. Close my eyes. They can take me. But I can't watch that creature hurt my children. Hurt Frank. If this is our fate, I will accept it now. Let it be over.

Then I hear the crackle of fire.

It's a stone building, unable to be completely destroyed. But these icy monsters can't abide the smell of the interior furniture burning. They retreat, dropping us on the floor. We moan, massaging our tailbones. I rush to my boys and wrap them in my arms.

"We need to get out of here," Frank says. "We'll die of smoke inhalation."

We go flying out of the upstairs, stopping only when we encounter obstacles. We climb over flaming furniture and curtains. We stick to the path, though I'm filled with fear. We could be going around in circles once more.

We reach the main hall and are about to blow through it when I see a group of exhausted people. Jay. Emil. The McMillans. We waste no time in getting to their staggering bodies, supporting them under our arms. It takes only a few trips, but we manage to get everyone out.

The night is gloomy and inky black. There is no moon, no lights to guide our way. I turn on my cell phone light, and we hustle all the survivors to their cars. I'm not sure that they can drive, but I underestimate them. They peel out faster than a racing driver reversing for another lap. Smoke pours from every orifice of the castle, cloudy and choking.

"Go, go, go!" I yell. Frank swings into the front seat and guns it.

But then I catch a flash of movement. Sitting near the castle as we speed by the front entrance. "Stop!" I yell again. "There's someone here!"

"No, let's just go!" the kids chime in. "We gotta go!"

Frank slows, though. Neither one of us can let a person stay here and die.

Winnie gets into the car, shoved against Anthony in the middle, who grumbles.

"The airport?" Frank says carefully.

She nods. Her face is streaked with tear stains, her makeup smeared, hair a tangled mess.

We drive in silence for a few minutes. My mind spins, eager to ask a hundred questions. I'm surprised when she volunteers the information herself.

"I'm sorry," she says softly, bending over her joined hands. "This wasn't supposed to be like this."

"What was it supposed to be like?" I reply. I'm trying to be kind, but my voice is edgy. We're still in the middle of nowhere, and who knew how far the creatures could reach. They'd invaded Nyla's dreams, after all.

"They promised me the show would be successful. If I let them feed on contestants. They'd only choose a few, they said. They'd find the people who brought them opportunity."

Like me. Like Jay. The entities had chosen us.

"I didn't know they were going to take people. Hurt them. Cause them to have those horrible visions." She sniffles. "They'll never leave me alone. Not till the day I die."

Anthony pauses his game and takes a moment to pat Winnie on the back.

"I'm sorry," she says. "They said it would be scary. Not like this."

"Everyone has a different definition of what's scary," I tell her.

"I never meant..."

I put up a hand. "Winnie. It's over. There's nothing more to say."

IT IS NEARLY dawn by the time we get home. The first thing I do is drop into the bed and fall asleep. My dreams are blissfully empty.

When I wake up, I'm more refreshed than I've ever been. I sit up, yawn, and stare out the window at the afternoon light. Frank is sprawled out next to me, still snoring.

I pad out to the kitchen and make coffee, then sit down on the couch. It's the middle of the week, but it might as well be a Saturday. Nothing has changed since then. Still nothing to wear, toys to pick up, dishes left all over. Trash on the floor.

But I carry this tiny piece of a dark heart. A sliver of valor for saving people I barely know. I would have sacrificed it all. My body taking a back seat to those of others.

I sit and stare at all of it, taking it in. Wondering what else I will give up before I destroy these creatures that have wrapped themselves around my mind, their tentacles driving hard into my brain.

I stand. Still in the clothes from last night.

I leave everything there and walk out into the fall sunshine.

MY STUPID TIME-TRAVELING GOLEM
OR WHATEVER

This is messy. And stupid. Who even cares—it's not like we are going to need these skills in real life. "Hey, Brandon, I need you to write a PowerPoint presentation about papier-mâché." Did I mention this is stupid?

The art teacher—Ms. Cranor, beloved by nerds, which I am decidedly not—strolls by. She's "supervising."

"Brandon, you haven't even mixed your flour and water yet." She clucks, pointing at my empty bowl. "You won't get far without your base."

She's such a genius. No wonder nerds love her.

Mackenzie Stoddard is sitting next to me, her hands already covered in nasty gloop. It smells like old bread. She's carefully wrapping newspaper around a wire figure. "Nice job, Mackenzie," Ms. Cranor says.

God. Girls. Always sucking up, unless they're in the back gossiping about who looks good and who needs to take a back seat.

I stare at the glass bowl in front of me. If I don't do something, Ms. Cranor is going to keep bugging me. Everyone else is already doing what they're supposed to.

Mackenzie side-eyes me. "Do you need an idea?"

"What? No." I curl my lip at her. "I just don't want to do this."

Mackenzie glances around. Ms. Cranor is across the room talking to another kid.

"No one does," Mackenzie whispers. She leans toward me, but with her hands occupied, it's like an awkward shoulder-bending thing. "But you want to get a good grade, don't you?"

I roll my eyes.

She fixes me with an "oh my God, Brandon" look. The same one I get from my little sister when I piss her off. Feels kinda good, actually. I run my hands through my bushy hair and rest my elbows on the back of the seat.

The seat catches on something behind me and tips. My head smashes on the floor, and pain rockets through my skull.

When I open my eyes, Mackenzie's gawking at me from above. Kids around the room are laughing and clapping. I'm in a daze until Ms. Cranor comes over and helps me up. Before I can protest, she pulls open one of my eyes. I can smell whatever peach body spray or deodorant she has on. "Oooh," she says. "We need to get you down the hall."

Ms. Cranor leads me down to the nurse's office. My head is spinning, and my hands feel clammy. I might throw up.

I hear the nurse on the phone trying to reach my parents. Good luck, lady. Neither one of them ever answers. They're both too busy with work. It's always been up to me and Julianne to take care of things at home, and it's not like the nurse is going to try calling my eleven-year-old sister.

"Well, if we can't reach your parents, I may have to have the principal sign off on transporting you to the hospital." The nurse is in front of me now. Where did she come from? And now I see two of her. Purple scrubs, blond hair in a ponytail, Crocs. Both nurses move back and forth in a dance as if I'm a snake and they're trying to charm me.

Oh, I'm definitely concussed.

I DON'T REMEMBER MUCH about the ride to the hospital other than I was in an ambulance. It was bumpy and cold. Too much air on my face. As soon as we got into the ER, the temperature changed, and my head started pounding. Now I'm lying in a dark hospital room with an IV in one arm and a barf bag in reach.

I'm not sure what time it is when Mom comes in. I just hear her voice. "Brandon?"

I groan in response.

"What happened?" She sits on the hospital bed next to me. Her skin is cold from outside.

"Art class accident," I mumble.

"Did you say art class?"

I let out another long groan. I feel so stupid.

"Oh, honey. They're going to keep you overnight, okay? I'll pick you up in the morning."

Mom stays for a little longer. It's nice when she holds my hand, like I'm a kid again and she's actually paying attention.

AFTER MY 24 hours in the hospital, I return to school.

I'm opening my canary-yellow locker to sling my bag inside when an object falls out from the top shelf. I duck, but when it's clear it's not going to make my concussion worse, I grab the item from the ground.

It's papier-mâché. But the surface is dried, hardened, covered in brown paint. It's hard to tell, but if I look at it from the side, it kinda looks like an animal.

I pick it up and stare at it.

"Yo, Kimball, you good?" A pack of guys passes me, throwing finger symbols and gestures at me. Nothing I recognize or care about. I don't even know these people. I smile and put up a peace sign. I can't tell if they're making fun of me or not.

Something feels wrong. Like I've been knocked into another universe. Like I am not the person who left here the other day.

We don't have art today. The special is gym, but I can't participate, so I sit on the sidelines watching my classmates shoot hoops and play dodgeball. I don't have my phone, so there's nothing to do but stare into nowhere.

I am really over school, I think. Kids race past me, colorful blurs. Girls are in a gaggle in the back corner, folding their arms and whispering. A few stragglers mill about, not wanting to get caught slacking but also unwilling to do much. I wonder what the point of it is. It's physical education, but there's no education part. Actually, I don't think I'm getting much education at all.

I start dissociating until I feel someone staring at me. I crane my neck, trying not to wrench it, and my gaze collides with Mackenzie Stoddard's.

Not her again. Jesus Christ. But she's already seen me.

She's in short shorts and sneakers. Never did I think goody-two-shoes Mackenzie could glam herself up like this. She doesn't have her glasses on, and her eyes are huge and lined like an anime character's. Not quite the same look as the other day.

"You okay?" She saunters up and takes a seat beside me. Did she always have these long legs?

"Uh, yeah."

Mackenzie hums. "That was pretty rough the other day."

"Yeah. Well. Nothing I can do about it now."

She jerks her head at me. "Are you saying you wish you didn't do it?"

Um, yeah? But based on the look on her face, I'm afraid to answer. She looks like she might stab me with a fork if I said I regret hitting my head on the art room floor.

Which is weird, but I do have a concussion.

"I mean... I just..."

Mackenzie's expression softens, and she drapes a hand around my shoulder. "It's okay. I know what you mean. And I'm grateful."

Her arm is an electric current. I sit up straight, back ramrod against the hard brick of the gym wall.

"You got my present, though, right?"

I don't think my brain is capable of doing math right now, so I'm unable to put two and two together. I stare at her.

"Silly." She pushes my shoulder. "I get it. You can't even hold a conversation now. We'll talk tomorrow in art, 'kay?"

The bell rings, and an army of kids heads for the locker room. I sit there like I am glued to the bench.

BEFORE I GET on the bus, I shove the brown papier-mâché critter in my bookbag.

Mom's car is in the drive when I get home. Not something you see every day. I push through the front door and yell for her.

She comes out of the kitchen wearing soft yoga pants and a hoodie. Her curly, bristly hair—like mine—is pulled on top of her head.

I blink. I'm seeing double again, like I did with the nurse. Only this time, I'm seeing two versions of my mom: the one in a tailored suit and a sleek chignon, the one I'm used to—and this one.

"Oh, good, you're home. I made you a snack." My mom holds out a plate with apple slices, cheese, and crackers. "How are you feeling?"

Confused, weird, messed-up… "Okay?"

She chuckles. "You don't sound too sure about that."

I put down my bookbag and blink. She's solidly Yoga Pants Mom. Who, to my knowledge, doesn't exist.

"I'm not used to seeing you home after work," I say.

My mom tilts her head like she doesn't know how to respond. Maybe she doesn't. I have no idea what the F is happening here except that Mackenzie put this thing in my locker and now my whole life is messed up.

Her laugh sounds forced. "That must be because you're always running to your room to play games right away."

Okay, she's not wrong about that.

I take the plate, set it on the kitchen table, and go to town on the snacks. Guess that's one good thing about this version of Mom.

As I chew, I think about the sensation in my belly. I have a hunch that this has something to do with multiple universes. Which is crazy because I've never heard of multiple universes before. I can feel my mind stretching to accommodate this information. When I close my eyes, my head pounds, and my stomach flips. It's all too much.

My sister Jules is eleven and gets off the bus an hour and a half after I do. I sit at the dining room table the whole time. After Mom called me out about my gaming—hell, she's not usually here, so what else am I supposed to do?—I didn't want to go upstairs and ignore her. And my brain is still rattling. Jules and I don't have the same kind of relationship most siblings do. We're pretty close. I think because we're always home together and have to keep each other company. I have to talk to her about this. While I spiral, Mom puts together another plate for Jules.

Jules arrives with her usual bang and slap through the door. She snags an apple slice and shoves it in her mouth.

"Hey," I yell across the kitchen. "How was school?"

She shoots me an acid look. "Like you care."

I deflate. Of course. This Jules is used to a mom that's always here. A mom that might even be... a helicopter parent.

Mom turns around and meets my eyes while Jules bangs her way up the stairs to her room.

Mom makes dinner. Dad comes home from work. He seems tired but more or less the same. Jules doesn't even come downstairs. I go up to my room. Seems like a pretty basic day with my bizarro family.

I don't have it in me to check my phone or check in with my gaming friends. They're going to be all different. So I just flop onto my bed.

Strangely, I can't tell the difference between this house and the one I'm used to. The same paintings on the walls, the same little decorations. As clean as usual. My room, too. My same gaming rig, same bed, same sheets and blankets. I have the same phone. If it weren't for everyone being batshit crazy, things would be normal.

Maybe I should go to sleep. Maybe I'll wake up and my parents will both be gone, and I'll be making sure Jules gets on the bus to before-care before I get on mine. And I won't know what version of my mother I'll find when I get home.

My phone beeps. I eye it warily. Still don't want to pick it up. But my curiosity gets the better of me, and I glance at the home screen.

Mackenzie?

Besides in art class, we've never talked—except for whatever the hell happened today. Her conversation was so confusing. She put her arm around me. What girl even does that? She mentioned a present. That weird papier-mâché thing.

I push the phone away and pad downstairs.

I scrabble in my book bag and pull it out. It's not too heavy, maybe half a pound, but my hand feels weighted down. It's sturdy, with a big chest and smaller legs. There's a round head without any eyes or nose. It could be some kind of animal or even a statue.

"Brandon?"

I'm still clutching the creature when I turn to see my mother. She's holding a book. A cup of tea rests on the end table beside her. I can smell whatever's in it, kind of flowery. The sky is growing darker in the windows behind her.

My mom—my real mom?—would not be reading. If she was even home. She would be on her computer, squinting at the screen.

"Hey, Mom," I reply.

"What are you doing?"

"Needed something out of my bookbag."

"What?"

What the hell. No reason to keep it secret from her if I'm in Bizarro World anyway. I turn and hold up the thing.

She unfolds her legs from under her and moves closer. I hold out the item, and she takes it. She gets a weird look on her face, almost disgust mixed with sadness. "Where'd you get this?"

"Uh, Mackenzie Stoddard made it? In art. The same day I fell over."

Mom runs her hands over the hard surface. "Since when do you refer to your girlfriend by her full name?"

I goggle. "Mackenzie's not my girlfriend."

"I had suspected that." She's still holding the critter, not meeting my eyes. A pit is growing in my stomach. "You don't know what this is, do you?"

I shake my head. I'm not part of reality anymore. I'm in some video game where I turned in the creature for a quest, and now I'm getting an explanation from an NPC.

Mom's voice has gotten softer. "You don't think she knocked you over, do you?"

My mind is going a hundred directions, but I try to focus on the question. Mackenzie was sitting right next to me. She could have kicked my chair or something. I don't remember. The concussion scrambled my memories. I shake my head.

"This is a golem," my mother says, moving closer to me so I can see it better. "They were first found in the fourth or fifth century in Jewish communities. Made out of common material, but can be animated by any source."

I stare. These words are not making sentences.

"I think she wanted to be your girlfriend," Mom continues. "She must have the gift of shaping time. The golem made it happen. And you having it continues the cycle."

I still do not get it.

"You're not my son," my mother says sadly. She moves to me and puts her hand on my shoulder. "You belong to a different Jacqui Kimball. And I don't know who's there to take her place."

MOM SAYS I should go to bed and we'll talk about it in the morning. Even if I'm not supposed to be here, I have to go to school.

But I lie awake, staring at the ceiling. The golem is in my bag, doing golem things, or whatever it does to keep me here. In another universe, I guess. A world where my mom stays home, Jules hates me, and Mackenzie Stoddard is my girlfriend.

Did she think I wouldn't find out? My phone screen shows ten missed calls, and my texts are blown up. *Where are you? Why won't you answer your phone? I'm worried. Brandon. Please call me.*

Why didn't she just ask me out? I wouldn't have said yes, but it would have been easier than forcing me into an entirely different universe.

Maybe she thought I wouldn't know. Maybe she thought the concussion would addle my brain so much that I wouldn't remember how things were before.

And why the hell can she "shape time" or whatever my mom called it? And why the hell does my mom know about such things? Is my mom in the X-Men?

More questions than answers. I stuff my pillow over my head and scream.

I GET DRESSED in a fog and drag myself down the stairs. Mom has a steaming mug of coffee with cream waiting for me. I accept it gratefully, the round sides warming my hands. We stand at the kitchen island in an awkward silence.

"I wasn't sure if you'd like it," she says finally. "But I figured you didn't get much sleep."

I yawn. "Not at all."

"You have questions."

I glance at the clock. "Not sure twenty minutes is enough time to cover them all."

"I should just explain." She looks down into her mug as if it's going to answer everything itself. "My family—our family—has a gift. It's called Time Seeking. We have the ability to see when time is being molded. Shaped."

I blink. "So that's a thing?"

I wonder if that's why I realized so quickly that I was not in the right universe.

"It is for me. I don't know if your version of your mother can do this. It doesn't sound like she's explained it to you."

I shake my head dumbly.

Mom-not-Mom comes around the corner and rests her hand on my shoulder. "I know you're not my Brandon, but I love you anyway. You can stay here as long as you want or as long as you need to. I can't change what's happened, but that golem can. As long as you're willing to confront Mackenzie."

THE GOLEM IS in my bookbag. Locked and loaded.

I can't help the anger that rises up in me as I walk into school. I'm more like stomping at this rate since I'm so pissed.

This world where my mom is sweet and my sister hates me—it isn't mine. And they want their version of me back, if they haven't figured out that the other me isn't me. God. This is confusing. This stupid freaking thing. I want to throw it across the hallway and bean Mackenzie right in her stupid face.

I check my phone (his phone). Twenty minutes till the first bell. I haven't read any of Mackenzie's messages. She can walk off a cliff. I'm done.

I find her at her locker. Her eyes are red and tears stain her cheeks. She turns to see me and only cries harder.

"What did you do?" I point in her face. "I'm not your boyfriend."

She sniffles. "I know."

"Then why?" I spread my arms to indicate the rest of the students plowing through the halls. "All these people are different, but you and I are from the wrong place?"

"I don't know. I don't know what I was thinking." She rubs a hand against her cheeks, swiping at the stains. "I guess I thought you would be different here and I would be the same."

"You gave me the golem." I grit my teeth. "It time-traveled me."

Mackenzie looks at the ground. "Well, we're actually in a different universe."

"I know that!" I yell. "But why?"

My shouting is turning heads. It's embarrassing, but if I can get back, no one will remember. Although here-Brandon might have a problem.

"Listen, this is the first time I tried to do this." She's full-on sobbing now. "And I liked you. And you thought I was some kind of goody-two-shoes, and you wouldn't have said yes, so I thought…"

"You're right. You're a nerd. I never would have gone out with you."

I want her to be upset. I want her to cry. I want to go home.

"Fine. Is it in here?" She grabs my bag, rips it off my shoulder. I don't even care if it will make things change again. Mackenzie plunges her hand in and pulls out the golem. I hate its blank face with no eyes. I hate its stupid, hard body. I want to throw it at her.

But instead, that's what she does to me.

The last thing I know is hitting my head on the floor.

~

I wake up in the hospital again.

No Mom, no Dad, no Jules. Alone.

When the nurse comes in, I ask her. "Have my parents been to see me?"

She shakes her head. "You're being kept overnight for observation. I assume someone will pick you up in the morning."

"What time is it?"

"Ten. Past visiting hours. It took you a long time to wake up. We'll need to roll you down to examination now."

They check a bunch of things. They ask me if I have a headache, am I nauseated, do my reflexes work. How tired am I. What do my pupils look like. A bunch of questions about my memory. What I remember from how I hurt myself.

"Girl at school pushed me," I tell them.

The nurse frowns down at my chart. "This says you lost your balance in a chair and hit the ground."

~

I don't have the golem anymore. Maybe Mackenzie still does. But whatever. I have to build another papier-mâché stupid thing.

Ms. Cranor isn't upset, though. "You had a bad fall," she says. "You'll need the extra time to finish."

I stare at the newspaper strips in the disgusting bowl, watching them marinate and feeling sick to my stomach.

"The concussion is making me nauseous." I look up at Ms. Cranor. "Can I do this next time?"

Mackenzie looks at me from across the room. Her seat's been moved at my request. I told Ms. Cranor that Mackenzie may have sabotaged my chair. Ms. Cranor's jaw went tense, but she moved Mackenzie all the same.

The bell rings, and we all put our stuff away. I have three more days to figure out what I want to make.

As we walk out into the hallway, teeming with kids, Mackenzie sidles up to me. I recoil.

She startles, rears back. "What did I do?"

How does she not remember?

I bet she does. I bet she's pretending. Ashamed of what she did to me. Maybe I haven't cut her enough slack. Maybe I was too mean to her.

Before I can say anything—if I was going to say anything—she turns away quickly as her face goes red. I watch her get lost in the crowd.

THE BOY AND THE CRONE

Crystal

I've always thought that by now, in my eighties, I would be a better writer. That I would be somehow bestowed with a gift from the muses. My words would flow with music. I'd write the kind of book the critics call "lyrical" and "astounding." I'd never been discovered in my twenties as I always wished, but I could be discovered now —the woman who kept her talent secret until she was near death.

Sadly, this has not come to pass. As I stare down at the city so far below me, hidden in my tower of unearned wealth, I can only write the same shit I've written my entire life.

My daughter is a shoe mogul. Of all things. She was a tomboy growing up and loved to play sports, especially basketball. Her designs, meant to improve players' agility and buoyancy, went viral: everyone's biggest dream in the twenties, no doubt. Now she is the owner and CEO, with little time for her mother. She is my only child, and my husband died years ago, struck with an aggressive form of blood cancer.

Tara's solution was to put me in a penthouse. We fled the US when the wars started, decamping overseas. Not that I'm safe at the top of a giant tower, but this country is known for its excess, this throwing about of money. I can order anything I want, have life brought to me on a plate. Occasionally, I even leave the building!

Not that I want to. Most days, I sit on the couch—ergonomically designed for a Person of a Certain Age—and write with my tablet and stylus. My arthritis doesn't make it easy, but I've never been one to use a sound recorder. Anything I say into a computer comes back wooden, uninspired.

I suppose that's how most of my writing comes out anyway, though.

Tara thinks I should submit my work. Agents, editors, literary journals—do they still exist? I've been out of the loop for so long. In my twenties, thirties, forties, I accumulated rejections, had email inboxes full of them. Occasionally I received requests for manuscripts, even had one company close to publishing me, but nothing ever worked out. I grew disillusioned.

It's hard to believe I don't have much time left. I still feel like a child most times. Thinking of all the stupid mistakes I've made in my life, everything I've thrown away.

Marco

The Giancasi Tower isn't built for kids.

The people who live here are mega-rich, semi-retired, coasting on old money. Marco sees them in the lobby, picking up their mail, wearing those slick hairbands that project hallucinations before their eyes. Pretending they're in a completely different world. Marco wonders how people can wish to escape real life when those lives are so perfect. Imagine being able to buy whatever you want, whenever you want. What luxury.

Marco is twelve and the son of Wyman, the doorman. He prides himself on leading the small group of employees' kids: Sheyna, Dahl, Ceriah, and any other randoms who show up to play. They range in age from seven to fourteen. Marco knows his father's colleagues don't want their children running underfoot. And their parents are busy working to pay the bills. So it's important that he carry this responsibility.

Sometimes the kids go outside, but the heat is brutal, and the Giancasi is one of the few buildings that can remain cold with robust air conditioning. The other businesses in town try their best, but they don't make it lower than eighty degrees Fahrenheit most days. It's slightly cooler at night, so they might play pickup basketball with the kids from the adjoining neighborhood—more staff kids from richy-rich apartments.

Today, they wake up super-early to gather in the lobby. Marco has instructed them to bring their swimwear, as they have access to the Giancasi pool, but only before the residents arrive. Sheyna is rubbing her eyes, throwing her hair into a stringy ponytail. She is the oldest, and each time he notices her breasts, he turns away.

Dahl, though—Dahl is shaky. He's nine, still such a kid, Marco thinks. Even though Marco is only a few years older, he feels wiser to the world and its workings. Maybe because he remembers being in the slums with his father. Maybe because he remembers his mother dying of heatstroke. Maybe because they wouldn't be alive if his father hadn't gotten the job here.

Marco puts a hand on Dahl's shoulder. "What's wrong?"

Dahl jumps at the touch as if Marco's hand is a spider. "I... I..."

"You what? Spit it out." This from Ceriah, the sassiest of the group.

"I saw her." Dahl cringes. "Mrs. Babbage."

They know her name from the time Dahl intercepted her mail. There was a package, and the return address was from Streak Shoes. The best shoes for basketball, no question. Dahl couldn't help himself —he had to take a look. But Marco's dad saw what was happening and called upstairs to the old crone.

Dahl had to apologize. He cowered below the stooped old woman, who snatched the box and growled at him. She'd placed the tip of her finger atop her nose and directed it straight at Dahl, then sneered, showing all her yellow teeth. He could only let his breath out when she got back on the elevator, still staring at him with those rheumy eyes.

Since then, Dahl's shoes have been cursed. He's clumsy, backing into things, falling over constantly. Once, he tripped, smashing his face on the ground and losing a couple teeth. His mother, who works in the kitchen, howled all the way to the emergency room. The hospitals are so crowded that they waited there for days.

His family can't afford a new pair, so he's constantly dancing around, doing his best to stay upright.

At Dahl's announcement, the kids begin to whisper, a hot buzz going through them. Marco puts up his palm for quiet. "Where did you see her?"

"Our apartment. I was the only one there," Dahl continues. "Dad was on early shift, and Mom was still asleep." He folds his arms. "I might have been fine if you hadn't made us come down here so early."

"So what, did you come out and she was there? She knock on the door? We need details," Ceriah says.

"I was leaving. She came down the hall."

"Why would she be on the third floor?" Marco has never seen the old lady outside of that single time, and he doesn't want to.

Sheyna reaches out and pulls Dahl under her arm. "Does it matter? He saw her. He's scared."

"Did she talk to you?" Ceriah asks.

Dahl shakes his head, his long hair flapping against Sheyna's torso. "I don't know if she saw me."

Sheyna hugs the boy more tightly. "Are you okay to go swimming? We don't want you to be scared."

Marco is starting to think Dahl is a big baby. But he wants to go to the pool. So instead of waiting, he marches off and scans his keycard to get in. They can come in or not. He doesn't care. Curse or no curse, he's not scared of some old lady.

～

Crystal

I was on the third floor when I spotted the boy.

I recognized him at once—the kid who was messing around with the shoes Tara sent me. Wyman had called me to come down and get it, and I was certain he was annoyed that I hadn't picked up the package yet.

The boy had handed me the box. His hands were trembling. I managed a smile, but he flinched, and I sighed inwardly as I headed back to the elevator.

Now he'd done the same after catching my eye in the hallway. Yes, I was moseying about on a different floor. The penthouse can be awfully stifling after a few days, and walking outside isn't practical. So I roam the halls, tracing circles in front of other people's doors.

I've always enjoyed children. As soon as my daughter was born, everything in my world changed. I had no desire to do anything other than dote on her. To give her one hundred percent of myself and more. Yet she wanted to be independent more than anything, and I had to let her go much sooner than I wished to.

I ride the elevator to the second floor. A change of scenery for my next lap around the building.

My boredom is so complete, so all-encompassing. I'm a terrible writer. I can't cook—one of Tara's personal chefs brings me my meals daily. I do like to read, but there are only so many books one can consume in a day. There's also the matter of my mistakes: things I repeat to myself, over and over. My cruelty to my husband as I neglected him to focus on Tara. Getting fired from my financial management job for overestimating a client's portfolio. Resorting to theft when we could barely afford to eat.

An idea strikes me as I pass the employees' quarters. I certainly do not need the money now that my daughter rolls in it. But I might benefit from supervising the employees' children. Babysitting, they used to call it. I could even send meals down for the couples to have date nights. I could be useful.

Excitement bubbles up in me as I get on the elevator and return to the penthouse. I grab my tablet immediately and navigate to the community bulletin board for the building. These posts are usually from residents: complaints about pets being too loud, speculation any time a medical van arrives, and gripes that there are so few food options in this neighborhood.

But I am going to make a useful post. I am going to bring something of value to the community here. Maybe make people happy. Get to know the children. Yes, this is my purpose at the end of my life. I will contribute. I will do something good.

Marco

After the pool, the kids are supposed to head back to their apartments for "school." This education consists of videos delivered by AI "teachers." Their assignments mean nothing, since there is no oversight of the "students." Society has all but given up on everything except surviving while the rich suck up the world's resources.

Marco makes a peanut butter and jelly sandwich, then projects his tablet on the wall to watch a show. It isn't long before he falls asleep, the exhaustion of the pool lulling him into a nap.

He wakes up to an insistent beeping. It's the tablet, glowing green with a notification. He sighs, rubs sleep out of his eyes. What could be so important?

The message is from Dahl. Marco rolls his eyes. This kid can be so dramatic.

My mom is going to farm me out to the old lady!

Marco frowns before typing back. *What the hell does that mean?*

They're leaving me with her so they can have a "date."

Also something Marco has never heard of. He types back two question marks.

It's where a couple gets to spend time together without kids.

Never heard of it.

Marco yawns. He can practically hear Dahl freaking out on the other side of the conversation, but he has no use for panic. His only goal is to figure out what he wants to do with his life. Yes, he's spoiled by the building, but he can't stay here forever. As much as his father wants to keep him from the wars, he might need to go fight. Become a medic, maybe. He's tired of being bored.

Man. She's going to eat me.

Marco laughs out loud. *Wtf?*

She eats kids. Ceriah told me. That's why they keep her locked in the penthouse. So she can't come downstairs and get us.

This makes no logical sense, especially considering Dahl has seen her twice: once by the mailboxes and once on the third floor. Marco says as much, and the dots that show Dahl typing start, then disappear, then start again. This continues for several minutes.

They must let her out sometimes, Dahl reasons. *For exercise.*

Marco chuckles. *Dude, you're gonna be fine.*

Then can you come with me?

Marco cringes as he steps around the couch and towards his father's snoring, sputtering face.

The sky is getting brighter outside their east-facing window. His father is working the evening shift today. Based on the empty bottles and discarded clothes surrounding the couch, Marco assumes his father got blasted and didn't bother to stumble into the bedroom. This is not a new occasion for Marco, but his father's smells and snorts repulse him.

His father's device lies on the ground, and Marco is grateful that he doesn't need to pull the thing out of a saggy pocket. He opens it and holds the screen to his father's face, praying that the ID software will work without his eyes open.

It takes him a few tries. Marco swears under his breath as the device beeps and whines. But when it happens, it's a heady feeling. Marco is in.

Clutching his father's device and his own keycard, Marco hurries to the first floor. Skaley is working the front desk, but he's too lost in his own screen to pay attention. Marco waves his father's barcode key to get inside the duplication room—well, more like the duplication closet.

It's a small, dark area holding a machine with a red barcode-reading light.

This is where they duplicate and deactivate keys. This is also where they allow permissions for barcodes in the staff apps. Marco knows he's going out on a limb with this and could get into deep trouble, but Dahl's safety is more important.

He scans his father's ID and presses the screen. *Copy.*

It takes only a second. *Copy to new card?*

He presses *Yes* and scans his keycard.

New credentials added to card.

Marco swallows.

MARCO WILL FOLLOW Dahl and the old woman up to her apartment. Since Marco now has the key—at least until his father catches him—he will sneak in a few minutes later. Dahl will have his device, so he can text Marco for a good place to hide. They know this plan is precarious, but it's all they can figure out to do.

Her apartment takes up the entire top floor, so Marco waits in a utility closet on the one closest to the top. He pulls his collar away from his neck. It's steaming in here. He keeps refreshing his device, waiting for Dahl's text. He is feet from the elevator, ready to move up at a moment's notice.

But the text never comes.

Thirty minutes or so go by—or has it even been that long? He has to get out of here. When he can't take it anymore, he pops out of the closet and heads for the elevator, going down, his heart thumping.

His apartment smells like booze. It's stone silent. His father hasn't picked up a single piece of trash or clothing from the floor. Marco sighs and puts his device on the kitchen counter. Then he starts to clean.

When it gets past eight and Dahl still hasn't texted, Marco begins to worry that the old woman has eaten him.

Marco sits with a bowl of popcorn watching some mindless nonsense on his device. He wonders: how could a woman even eat a kid in a building like this? Dahl's parents would notice he was gone, and with her apartment being the last place the boy went, the old woman would come under suspicion. Unless she has some kind of magic that would put a veil over everyone, convincing them Dahl never existed.

Marco's blood chills at that thought. He talks to Dahl every single day, looks out for him like a brother. He supposes that if the woman uses magic, Marco won't even remember Dahl. She could erase Marco's memories And that's the worst part of it—who else could take Dahl's place in Marco's past?

The door creaks open, and Marco startles. It's his dad, of course. Dahl wouldn't come to the apartment.

But then, the smell wafting in isn't of booze or even the stark scent of floor cleaner. It smells dank, nasty. Like the person approaching him is rotting.

A person? Or a... something?

His heartbeat quickens.

Marco pulls a waffled blanket over his head. He can see through the knots his mother knitted so long ago.

He waits for the door to come fully open, but it never does.

Crystal

It's so nice to have the boy as company.

At first, he seemed frightened. Uncomfortable. Which I can understand. When I was young, we were scared of older folks too. We couldn't possibly know what their lives were like with all those decades between us. Now that I'm here, I think back to how that used to be. Our grandparents lived through the wars and the introduction of television. But now we are such old fools, all of us who grew up with floppy disks and computers that didn't connect to the Internet. We never thought this would happen to us.

Dahl had clutched his device. "Would you mind if I played on this?" he said in a small voice.

"Oh, certainly," I said. "But don't you want to spend time with me?"

He could only sputter in return. "Uh... sure?"

Now we're playing an old board game on my dining table. There is no real dining room, only a spot beside the kitchen, but it's enough room to display the board and pieces. At first, Dahl goggled at it, saying he'd never seen something like it before. But once I taught him how it worked, he was as excited as any kid I'd known back in the day.

"Sorry!" he calls out as he knocks over one of my red tokens.

I laugh. "I'll get you next time."

When he tires of the game, we talk about his life. School, his friends, and all those matters. He asks me what school was like when I was young. I sigh as I reminisce. "It's not like it is now, online," I tell him. "We all went to buildings. The weather... it wasn't this hot. We played outside in the grass. Sometimes it rained."

He gasps, a little-kid gasp showing mild surprise. "Rain? Really?"

"You betcha."

Dahl shakes his head. "You're so..."

"Old?" I prompt.

"No..." He apologizes all over himself. "Sorry, I mean, uh... you're not what we thought you would be."

I adjust my long skirt under the table and sit forward. "What did you think I would be?"

"Well, Marco, he said..." The boy's cheeks go bright red. "Uh, I should..."

I hold up a hand. "It's okay, honey. I understand why I might be scary to you."

"But you're not." He looks at the floor. "I mean, now I know you're not."

I deliver him to his parents' apartment as promised. They look delighted—refreshed, even. I have done a good deed.

Dahl turns as he steps into the doorway. "Can we hang out again, Mrs. Babbage?"

I can't help smiling. "Of course, dear."

On my way back upstairs, I think about that other child. Marco.

Really, I'm concerned about all those children, the ones glued together. Dahl has broken away to get to know me, but Marco is still the ringleader. Dahl seemed almost scared of the older boy. I wonder what ticks in that boy's head. What makes him seek power.

I don't know what true power is. My husband was the head of our family, and my daughter was the one who sought success. As I get older, though, I find that I want a taste of it. I could never succeed with my writing, could never evolve from this mundane wife and mother I was. The only time I felt on top of the world was when I was siphoning thousands of dollars from my employer's coffers, and even then my victories felt hollow when it was all over. Even though I'd never been caught.

And now there's not much left to me at all.

Meddling in the affairs of children? *What a waste of time,* my husband would have said. *It's too late to change.*

What am I changing into, though?

Marco

He wakes up on the same couch his father crashed on last night. The sun is blinding in his face. His father must have slept in his normal bed.

He blinks out his overnight tears and sweat and rubs his eyes. Then he remembers—Dahl. The group. They'll be awaiting his guidance.

Marco rushes into the bathroom and palms water onto his face. He doesn't know what it's like to wake up hung over, but he can imagine it, and that imagination feels a lot like this. Sufficiently cleaned, he searches for his device. It's behind a pillow on the end of the couch, and he snaps it up.

No messages. Not from the team, not from Dahl.

That woman. Marco grits his teeth. And this is all because Dahl's parents "wanted a dinner date." Which he still doesn't get.

He taps out a message to the group. *Meet downstairs in twenty?*

No one responds.

Marco does, in fact, show up in the lobby in twenty minutes. He finds a spot on the waiting chair by the front door. Every time someone comes through, there is a blast of heat on his face. They can't go swimming today, not after sleeping in so late. But they can study together or play some games on their devices. There are some options.

As he sits, though, he becomes more and more uncomfortable. No one comes. Did they not get his message? Marco sifts his device from his pocket and checks the IP. No, no one has even opened it, but the texts all delivered. They hated him enough to ignore him?

A tear slides down Marco's cheek. It is like Dahl has left. Along with everyone else.

Unless...

Marco's stomach aches.

Dahl could be gone for good.

Crystal

The next day, Dahl skips up to my apartment. "Look what I did in art class!" he calls out, brandishing a small clay sculpture. It is round and gray, and I have no idea what it is.

"Very nice," I say.

"I want you to have it." Dahl bounces to my windowsill and places the object on it. "As a thank you for being awesome."

My heart melts. It's what I always wanted to hear from my daughter. But by the time she was nine or ten years old, she wouldn't say those things anymore. It was all about her rise to fame, the business she built, and later, the empire.

"You're welcome. Really, you shouldn't have done that."

"I should have!" The boy crosses his arms. There's a tiny gap between his front teeth. "I wanted to."

"Well, thank you," I say playfully. "That was very kind of you. Do you want to come in? I'll make you some tea."

Dahl hesitates. I study him further. His cheeks are plump and round, his hair a fuzzy blond mess, his eyes a stormy gray. He's at that age where he's still sweet and cute, still not jaded by the world outside. He doesn't know how horrible things have become, even after the little bit I've told him about my past. I should tell him to go. I don't want to make things weird.

"I just…" He drags a toe across the carpet. "I don't know what tea is."

I chuckle and feel my face spread in an unbidden smile. "Well, my dear, let me show you. I promise I won't bite."

WE SIT over cups of steaming chamomile. Dahl confirms that he likes it, although it's a little hot for his liking. I ask him how his day was, besides his art class.

"It was okay." Dahl stares into his mug. "I feel weird telling you."

I lean forward. "Why's that? I know we're only new friends…"

"Yeah, I guess that's it."

He looks up, and I catch his eye straight on. I see him cringe for just a second, and I hate my age. These children are supposed to be my second chance. To help where I couldn't with Tara.

"You can trust me," I say. "But you don't have to tell me. Is there someone else you trust? It seems like this is bothering you."

Dahl takes a gentle sip. "It's Marco."

Again? "Is everything okay?"

"He texted everyone this morning and asked about getting together." Dahl sighs. "No one wants to do this crew thing anymore. We set up another group chat."

I had my own teen drama. I was on the volleyball team, and we iced out this girl named Isabella, and I don't even recall why. I just remember her sitting on the sidelines in tears, and the rest of us were so callous that we didn't care. Seems that hasn't changed in seventy-plus years. And this boy is so much younger than I was then.

I'm intrigued, though.

Marco

Marco can't stand being in his smelly apartment alone. He carries his device and earbuds downstairs to the building's library.

There are a few small tables, some reading chairs, and a curtain drawn over the window. Marco turns on the lamps even though he could easily let light in from the outside. He doesn't want to keep the sun company right now.

He's slumped over an algebra video when he senses a presence in the room.

It's Sheyna, carrying her own device. Her eyes widen, and she turns to step away.

"Wait." Marco pulls out an earbud. "Hey. You don't have to leave."

She pauses. "I don't want to bother you."

"You're not. Come on, we'll just hang out together while we study."

Her jaw clenches just a little. "No, it's okay."

"Sheyna, wait." He puts out a hand. There's a swirling in his stomach like he's going to cry. "Is Dahl okay?"

"As far as I know."

Marco's unconvinced. Dahl's silence can only mean the old woman has devoured him. But the rest of them...

"Can you stay for a minute?" he asks Sheyna. "I need to know what I did."

Marco can tell she doesn't want to say anything. But he holds her gaze, and she cracks.

Sheyna sits down across from Marco and places her device on the table. "Look, man. No one wants to hurt your feelings. But the way you talked to Dahl the other day..."

He furrows his brow. "What do you mean?"

"About the old lady." Sheyna looks down, runs a finger along the track of the wood table. "He was scared out of his mind."

"Well, she's scary." Marco can feel the rage getting hot inside him, but he tamps it down.

"Yeah. But she isn't some kid-eating monster."

He side-eyes her. "You sure about that?"

Sheyna blows out her breath. "Come on, Marco. Be real."

"You guys didn't have to freeze me out. I'm the leader. You could be straight with me."

She laughs. It's almost a scoff, like she's making fun of him. "The leader? There's no leader. No follower. We're all the same, man. We're all trying to make it here. And you were mean. No one wants to be around a mean guy."

"I'm being real!" Marco's blood is simmering. He's getting louder. "You all needed to know what kind of danger that lady is. Sometimes you have to face hard truths."

"Yeah," says Sheyna as she gets up and makes for the door. "Yeah, you do, Marco."

BACK IN THE APARTMENT, it's all he can do not to slam his device on the floor. But they don't have money for another one, and if he wants to make any new friends, he's going to have to go online.

Marco hates the idea. Surfing around looking for an Internet pen pal. It's not like he's been a tyrant to them. All he was doing was keeping them vigilant. Keeping them safe. That's—that was his job.

The front door bangs open. Marco's body tenses. It's his father, dressed for work, but his tie is askew and he's sweating.

"Marco!" his dad roars.

"I'm right here." Marco sits up. "What's wrong?"

"Did you copy my key?"

A chill goes down through his back. He's frozen. Can't think of a credible lie.

"You know there are cameras everywhere." His father's eyes are wild. "The board came to discipline me. I'm a step away from getting fired, Marco. And then what would we do?"

Marco's lips open and close, but he can't speak.

"Answer me," his dad yells.

As he comes closer, Marco can smell the booze on his father's breath. Marco balls his fists. He knows he won't be able to control himself much longer.

"Yes, I took your device. Yes, I made a key." Marco grits his teeth, but he can't remain calm. "I did it to make sure my friend would be okay."

"What, did you think you would break into his apartment?"

"No, I—"

"I got written up, Marco. You know what that means? Next time it won't be a pardon. Do you want to live on the street? Or die on the street? Because I wouldn't be able to get another job, you know that?"

"Do you think your drinking has anything to do with that?" Marco rolls up onto his feet. "You're always smashed. And I can smell it on you. You're not sober at work, you know."

Even in the dim light, Marco can see every hair on his father's chin, every yellow tooth. A terrible smell envelops them.

His father rages, flailing out, his fists on their way to Marco's face. Marco ducks. His body coils. He'll defend himself no matter who's coming at him.

There's a light tap on the door. Then louder.

Marco steps back. His father pitches forward, rolls down over the couch.

"Hello?" calls a gravelly voice.

His father stumbles to his feet, as if remembering his place. He brushes down his coat and pants. Marco's veins are still pounding.

His father opens the door. "Yes, ma'am?"

"So sorry to disturb you," the old woman says. "But is Marco home?"

～

HE TRAILS the old lady into the elevator.

How could his dad do this? Send him off to his own doom, especially after Marco's best friend has just disappeared? And Sheyna was worried about Marco being mean to Dahl. None of that shit matters when people are dying. And all because of that one old lady.

How will she do it? Will she hit him over the head? Knife him?

Poison him? No, his body wouldn't be of use to her if it wasn't edible. Would she boil him alive? No, he'd scream and someone would come. Maybe.

Her apartment's dark. Marco recognizes that fusty smell, the one that followed him downstairs, the one that crept at the apartment door. She claps her hands, and the lights come back on, and he can see her in the full light all at once.

She has on a loose jumpsuit-thing that drapes across her chest and turns into pants. Her gray hair is twisted up behind her head, and she has lipstick on. She doesn't even look like the woman who came to his door just twenty minutes ago. She looks... normal.

"You can call me Crystal," she says. "Have a seat."

He doesn't move.

"Look, Marco. We both want the same thing. We're alike, you and I. We need to talk this out."

"I can't trust you," he says.

"I can see why you would feel that way–"

"You took my friend."

Crystal pauses, and Marco knows he's got her. She'll confess now. He's amped from the almost-fight with his dad, and he can pummel this old crone.

"He's confided in me, yes."

"But where is he?" Marco hears a note of wheedling in his own voice, and he feels his neck turning red. "I haven't heard from him since before he came here. And no one else is talking to me either."

"He's at home. He's fine."

"Can you prove it?"

"Call him," the lady says mildly. "Or why don't I do it. Computer— call Dahl Jensen's room."

The ringtone goes off. Marco is a statue.

"Hello?" comes his friend's little voice.

"Oh, hello, sweetheart! It's me, Mrs. Babbage. Checking in on you!"

"Hi!" Marco has to admit that Dahl sounds happy. "It's nice to hear from you!"

"Well, dear, I'll call you back later, okay? I just wanted to make sure you were alright."

"I'm fine, Mrs. Babbage! Bye!"

The call chirps off, and a thick silence fills the room. Crystal is looking pointedly at Marco.

Marco sighs and sits down.

"Do you want a cup of tea?" she asks.

He shakes his head. He's still not going to eat or drink anything she offers him.

"Can we talk about this?"

"I guess," he mutters. He supposes he's not getting out of here until they "talk."

"I'll get down to the point of it, then." Crystal arranges her hands on her lap. "Dahl is afraid of you. I wouldn't normally intervene at this point, but you two are best friends. He needs you in his life."

"Afraid of me?" Marco startles. "Why?"

"Well." Crystal's lips twitch. "You made him afraid of me."

Marco squirms on the old woman's uncomfortable couch. He wonders how anyone, even back in the day, could sit on this.

"I'm sorry," he chokes out. "If that offended you, I'll—"

She puts up a hand. "Like I said. You and I are the same."

His voice comes out quiet. "How do you mean?"

She pauses. "We both have what we do not want. And we want what we do not have."

He blinks.

"Power," she says. "And purpose."

He swallows. The weight of it all lands on his shoulders. She may not be wrong.

"I know. It's hard to understand," she says softly, moving toward him, almost like she might touch him. Devour him.

Marco jumps up, fire in his feet, and runs.

～

Crystal

I curl up on the couch with my notebook and face the east window.

Both boys are at home, safe in their beds. I hope they're dreaming.

I need to stay away from the kids for a while. My heart is rattled by all this. I never meant to be someone scary. But this is what aging has made me.

I stare down at the blank notebook, then look outside. The darkness is broad and empty. Artificial light sparkles from the buildings, trailing across the pervasive smog that buries the city. I am so far away from all that.

My pen skids across the tablet with looping, unnecessary words. My writing hasn't gotten better. I haven't changed. I'm here, sitting up in my tower, looking down on the world that never wanted me.

I get up and amble into the kitchen, conscious of my shuffling feet. The teapot sits on the stove. I open the fridge and peer inside. Tara and I are vegetarians, and my shelves explode with produce that she has provided for me.

I made that girl, I think.

She actually answers when I call. Maybe because it is so late. She barely sleeps, my daughter, but we all know that everything slows down in the small hours.

"Hey, Mom. What's up?"

Tara always sounds rushed, though.

"Nothing. I wanted to hear your voice."

She laughs. "That's an odd thing to say."

"Is it really, though?" I laugh back. "You're my kid." I picture her young face, her plump cheeks. Her messy blonde hair. A speck of chocolate on her mouth.

"Guess I am. What's going on?"

"Nothing, I said. Maybe try 'how are you.'"

"How are you?" Tara tries.

"I was just thinking that I appreciate you taking care of me." I bite my lip. "I saw all that food in the fridge…"

"Yeah, of course, Mom. I'd do anything for you."

A tear wells up, and I swipe it away.

"You ever try a burger?"

Tara giggles. A sound I haven't heard in decades. "What?"

"A burger. I don't know, I've been kind of curious about it. Now they have those lab-grown ones…"

She sounds puzzled. "I thought we were vegetarians because meat is bad for you."

"I mean, yes, but the main reason was because I didn't like animals dying."

"Huh," Tara says. "I never knew that."

"So you want to try getting that lab-grown stuff for me? Maybe we could eat together."

"I'm sure Boris could come up with something." Her laugh tinkles through the phone again. "Mom. You're acting sorta weird today."

"Yeah," I agree. "I kind of am."

"I like it, though." Her voice softens. "I'll call you tomorrow."

My whole body goes limp. "I'd like that."

I give up on the notebook and head to bed, bringing my device with me. I'm about to pull up a book, but my finger wiggles against the screen. I suddenly feel so light, so valuable. I put it down and roll back into the warm set of pillows and sheets. And then, nothing.

SAVE THE KIDS

I idle in the library parking lot waiting for my ex to hand over the kids. The place is closing, and people eye my car as they walk out to leave. I must seem suspicious, staying too long after the librarian turns off the sliding doors and locks them shut.

I pull down my sunglasses and stare out through the windshield. I'm parked in front of a copse of trees, where sparrows flit from branch to branch.

He pulls into the lot just as my dash clock flips to six. Mellie and Teagan pile out of his back seat and into mine. My girls smell like sweat and sand, and I feel a rush of love. "Did you have fun?" I ask them as I adjust my mirrors.

"Yeah," they chorus.

"We're tired," Mellie adds.

"I would be too. It was a long day."

I'm about to reverse out when Jack appears next to me. I resist the urge to roll my eyes but roll down the window instead.

He bends down to look at me. "You haven't responded in the chat yet."

In the twenty years I've known Jack, he hasn't changed a bit. More weathered, a bit grayer at the temples, but male pattern baldness has spared him. He's always been smoking hot, emitting pheromones that drag women into his orbit.

My jaw clenches. "I'm not sure about my schedule."

"You need to get sure about it. The gig is next Friday night and we don't have much time to rehearse."

I tense at the blatant mansplaining. "I know that. It'll be fine."

"Okay. Well. I don't feel fine about it. But once you pick a time, maybe I'll feel better."

And this is why we're not together anymore.

"Okay, Jack," I say again. "I will text soon."

MOST PEOPLE in town know who I am. Know who we are. Save the Kids had some bangers in the late aughts. Besides, it's not like I can hide my white Volvo EV when I'm also involved in school volunteering and civic events in between gigs.

People know Jack and I are divorced. It's gossip. One might call it celebrity gossip if we were considered celebrities anymore. We took breaks for our kids to be born and then for our epic divorce. We still get booked, but not like we used to.

I actually have a PTA meeting on Monday night. One of the officers contacted me to see if I would like to join. It'll be new, but I'm kind of excited. Hard to believe school is starting again. The girls were already moaning until I told them I'd take them shopping at the outlets tomorrow. Mellie is fifteen, Teagan thirteen, and there's nothing they love more than Stanleys and Starbucks.

As expected, they glue themselves to their phones as soon as we get home, but at least they're downstairs in the family room with me. I hang up my purse—Coach, classic, just Midwestern enough—and choose a spot on the overstuffed gray couch. My Cornish Rex, Fiona, jumps into my lap right away, and I run my fingers over her brindled hair.

Once Fiona gets bored and removes herself, I reach for my laptop, which is beside me on the couch. I order pizza so I can get back to business, then open my composition software. I've been tearing my hair out over this new song all day, and I want at least a draft before the next rehearsal. The one Jack won't stop bothering me about.

The notes seem to run into each other. Chords don't make sense. Lyrics aren't quite there. I need to get to the piano keyboard, which is currently littered with coffee cups from my all-day writing session. But I can't drag myself up from where I sit. Even though they're tapping on their phones, engrossed in whatever they're doing, I want to be with my girls. I'm not myself when they aren't with me.

I know better than to ask them how their days were and what they did. They'll tell me in their own time, after they eventually tire of the allure of whatever their friends are doing. Now is the time for me to back off, to let them find me when they need me.

Sure enough, pizza arrives, and I slap my laptop closed. Teagan rushes to the door to collect the food. We eat from paper plates around my four-top dining table. "I'm glad to be home," Teagan sighs over her veggie lovers' slice.

Mellie nods. "Me too."

Jack's place isn't home for them. I feel bad about it, but it's just true.

I fork salad into my mouth. "What else did you do with Dad?"

Mellie shrugs. She's wearing a tee with ripped shorts and gladiator sandals, and her straight brown hair is tied up behind her ears. She's such a cool kid, not in a trendy or preppy way. She's easy. I don't know how she got that way, since Jack and I are both so Type A.

"Not a whole lot," Teagan chimes in. She's my mini-me and has inherited my compulsions, but Mellie does help rein her in. The girls are close. "We had a barbecue."

I wait to see if either of them will mention Jack's girlfriend, but they know better.

"Dad's in his office a lot," Mellie notes. She takes a small, delicate bite of a breadstick. "He's writing something for the band."

I stiffen. "News to me."

Mellie makes a face. "Sorry. I figured you would know."

"Dad hasn't written anything in years."

The girls exchange glances. As if I'm Mount Florence and they don't know whether I'm going to blow.

"I don't know, Mom," Mellie says with a half-shrug. "Maybe he just felt inspired."

~

Our rehearsal space is at Jack's house. Not my first choice, but it was our marital home, and we'd had the studio custom built. It didn't make sense to rehearse anywhere else. My condo is twenty minutes away. I wish I could run from him, but the girls need to stay at The Barlow School, and we're still coworkers. I'm counting down the days till I can retire.

After taking the girls shopping, I'd holed myself up with my keyboard and agonized over the song. It had to be done by tonight's Sunday rehearsal. I wasn't going to let my ex outdo me.

Jack and I had bonded over the fact that we were both driven, performance-minded, and expected nothing less but success. Our relationship was a lit match tossed into gasoline. We were obsessed with each other until we agitated each other. The kids didn't fix our marriage. But nothing could break up the band, and here we were.

I flip a wave to our drummer, Tad, and pull the chord sheet from my bag. Of course, we never perform with paper in front of us, but I'll need it until the notes get under my fingers. It's only gotten harder to remember as I get older.

Jack and his girlfriend swan in as I'm noodling around. Mariah became our bassist after our previous one stepped aside. I knew from the minute she joined that he'd fall for her. She was stunning, for one, and much younger than us. And she was good. Talent was Jack's biggest aphrodisiac.

He takes up his guitar and leans over my shoulder. As reluctant as he may be to leave Mariah, he and I have always sung harmony together. It's part of our brand. And people are fascinated that we still play music together even after a discordant split.

It is the one thing we do well.

"No wonder you didn't want to schedule rehearsal." I feel the heat off his body. "Working on something?"

"I could say the same to you." I flutter my fingers across the keys, finding chords here and there.

He grins. "They can't keep anything to themselves."

I crane my neck to look at him. "Do they have to? This is still our band, right?"

Jack scoffs and waves a hand, letting his guitar drop and swing from his neck. "It's just a new song. No big deal."

"You never write though."

"I have something to say." Jack cocks his head at my music. "Clearly you do too."

My new piece is a holy disaster. I start by laying out the chord sequence, then add in the interest and the vocals. Normally everyone else would join in when it seemed right, but I'm alone, my voice warbling atop my clumsy fumbling. I clear my throat, reach for some water, and say it before anyone else can. "Needs some work."

No one agrees with me, because agreeing when someone is self-deprecating is the worst, but it's obvious.

"Let's just run through the set," Tad says, checking his Apple watch. "School starts tomorrow. I need to make sure my kids are ready."

"Yeah, us too," I say. Jack and Mariah both nod, and I grit my teeth at the thought of Mariah "getting ready." The girls will be at my house, anyway. I'll be taking their first day of school pictures.

We run the set with only minor squabbling over intonation between Jack and me. Mariah looks smug as usual, so I don't watch her at all. It's not like the bass line does anything interesting unless she has a solo, and even then I just stare at my keys.

I'm ready to zone out until Jack speaks up. "I've been working on something."

"You have accompaniment?" I ask him, stretching my back. God, it hurts.

"This is just me solo." He starts strumming, finding his way into the song, then quietly adds vocals.

I stare in disbelief as I hear the words of a love song. *True and clear...*

the love I'd never fear... you're the world in a glass globe... you're everything I'd never owe.

They don't make much sense, but neither does Jack most of the time.

When he's done, he lets the guitar go and digs a ring box out of his pocket.

"Jesus fucking Christ," I huff and make my way out before I can see how much he spent on that bullshit.

MONDAY EVENING, I slink into the PTA meeting late. I don't want anyone to think I'm too eager.

The woman who invited me, Patricia Richards, is at the podium up front. She's as chic as one would expect: denim jacket with a striped tee, blonde hair in a sleek bun. The library is full but not crowded; Barlow is a small school. It's K-12 and my kids have gone here ever since we moved back to Ohio, but I'd never spent much time involved with the group itself. I've mostly helped the music teacher with demonstrating instruments and putting together crafts for the art classes.

The truth is—I need friends. The life of a washed-up folk singer isn't glamorous, but I would settle for slightly interesting.

I scan the room for anyone I might know. The women near the front are so fucking beautiful. I'm no slouch—I take good care of myself— but they look otherworldly. Rich husbands, no doubt. Behind them are eager beavers, probably parents of kindergarteners ready to start micro-managing their impressionable children's lives. I fixate on a woman with bouncy red curls and freckles and wonder if she'll have perfectly straight hair by spring.

"Thank you all for coming." Patricia's voice is pleasant, melodic. "Let's do some housekeeping first. If you haven't paid your dues, you can Venmo Annie Vane. There will be a link to Annie's information in the email recap from today."

Everyone nods. Annie waves her hand above the crowd. Another beautiful face—she resembles a young Demi Moore, her eyes pools of black.

"We'll also take volunteers for committees," Patricia continues. "The most crucial being the Fall Festival."

A male throat clears. I turn with a jolt to see my ex-husband sliding into the row behind me, accompanied by Mariah. My guts are roiling as I will myself not to stare. Especially at that glittering diamond, illuminated by the fluorescent lights.

"Do we have to volunteer for that now?" asks the redhead in the front. She's holding a notebook and her pen is poised above the paper. It's almost charming but mostly pathetic.

"No, we'll send a SignUp Genius. But thanks for the question!" Patricia smiles mildly. "I'll go over the needs. We have two months to plan, although last year's committee has done much of the work for you."

I start to zone out as she lists group tasks. Outreach, sales, catering, decorations... Maybe I should have stayed home.

"And for the entertainment, I've invited our local celebrities." Patricia beams in my direction, and a rock drops in my stomach. "Jack and Florence Ridley from Save the Kids are here!"

Everyone claps. What the fuck did I agree to? I swivel my head back toward Jack and Mariah, but they look as clueless as I feel.

"As you know, Teagan and Mellie Ridley have attended school here since they were in the lower grades. But now that they are both with the upper school, which the Fall Festival directly benefits, I felt it appropriate to invite their parents. Let's have a round of applause for them!"

More clapping. I want to become part of my uncomfortable chair.

As the meeting breaks up, I turn to Jack before he can leave. "Did you tell anyone we would play at this thing?"

He shakes his head. Mariah inches closer to him.

"So they assumed." My face flushes. I'd thought I was being invited to the PTA because someone wanted me there, but Jack got an invitation too. They wanted our dues and our band. I'm surprised this hasn't happened years earlier.

"I don't think there's any harm in it," Jack says. "If it will help the school raise money."

"I don't know." I fiddle with the strap on my crossbody bag. "Someone should have asked us."

"That could change." Jack grabs Mariah's arm. "Come on, let's go."

I goggle at him. "You don't care?"

They both shrug.

As the room clears out, I approach the head PTA lady. President, I guess. I run my hands back over my smooth hair and wait for her to exit a conversation with another person. When she finally turns to me, I pause.

"You don't need to introduce yourself. Thank you for coming, Florence." Patricia reaches for my hands and holds them in hers. Her perfect manicure lays against my old and crusty nails. I haven't been to the salon in a few months, and my polish grew so far out that I had to use a nail file to remove the gel.

"I'm just wondering about the Fall Festival. We've never been, and..." I consider my words carefully even though I know they'll be awkward no matter what I say. "You expect Save the Kids to play?"

Patricia's response is calm. "Of course. The festival is our biggest fundraising opportunity with the upper school. Why wouldn't I ask?"

"You didn't ask, though." I think of my poor, neglected song. "We may have another gig."

"Your ex-husband assured me you didn't. He said your schedule was open."

Well, we have the Beachland Ballroom Friday, and the Agora next week, but sure. We'll fit in a concert we won't even get paid for.

I put on my most saccharine voice. "I have to tell you," I begin. "Don't ever listen to Jack when it comes to the kids. Don't listen to Mariah either. She's not their mother. I would appreciate a heads up when you speak to them."

Patricia doesn't look alarmed. "Doesn't your husband deserve privacy, as you do?"

"Not when it comes to the kids." I turn on my heel, then look back. "Or to the band."

THE REDHEAD IS SITTING outside the building on a wooden bench near Barlow's impeccably kept gardens. Her eyes are on her phone screen, so I won't bother her. But then I see how red her face is, and her dried tears.

I stop and lay a hand on her arm. She jumps at the touch. "I'm sorry," I say. "Are you alright?"

She turns her face up to me. "I mean... you don't want to hear about it."

"Try me." I stick out my hand. "I'm Florence."

"Briar." She wrinkles her cute nose. "My parents thought they were cool."

"You kidding? I got called Aunt Flo all throughout middle school."

Briar snorts. I take that as an invitation to slide beside her.

"I know who you are," Briar says.

I nod. "Most people around here do."

"It must be awkward to work with your ex, huh?"

I think about how Jack and I have to sing so closely in tune. How I have to lock in to wherever he is just to keep our sound working. How I have to force that flame to flicker, to fan it, bring it alive just long enough to energize our music. Mariah's bass there the whole time, driving, reminding me none of it is real anymore.

"Yeah," I say. "Do you have an ex?"

"How did you know?" Briar looks up and gestures with her phone. "He was supposed to take the twins this weekend so I could go on a date. I mean, my first date since we broke up more than a year ago, and of course he's already got a live-in girlfriend since they were seeing each other before we even got divorced. Now he's going to see some band with non-refundable tickets, and he claims he didn't know he was supposed to take them. I can't count on him for anything."

She hangs her head, and I pat her on the back. Briar wears a denim jacket similar to that of the PTA princesses, but it looks more real on her. Like she's a normal person, not airbrushed into the model of a put-together paragon of a woman.

"Hey, I know we just met, but do you want me to take them?"

Briar raises her head. "Are you kidding me?"

"I mean, you know I'm not an axe murderer. I've been on TV."

"I've seen you in concert. Before you guys…" She puts up her hands as if she's going to offend me. "I saw A Particular Melancholy in 2004."

"Are you kidding? That's awesome!" I lean back, feeling a little cheered. It was getting close to eight, and the air was cooling off enough to be comfortable. "I miss them."

"Whatever happened to Phillip the Masked? They said he ran away and never came back?"

I shake my head. No, he never did. But I like to think that he gave me that chance because he knew I needed it. Keyboard alone doesn't make a star, not even if you're Tori Amos or Fiona Apple. Or whatever other piano queens there are now—I don't keep good enough track. My voice, tangled with Jack's, is what made us famous.

"So are you convinced I won't axe-murder your kids?" I look at Briar's pretty green eyes. "I'm serious. You should do this for yourself."

Her shoulders relax. "You are too kind. Really. I owe you so much."

"Don't even think about it." I gesture for her phone. "C'mon, I'll put in my details."

A FEW DAYS LATER, I'm getting ready for rehearsal to start, tapping out a melody on the keyboard. I think I've identified the problem. Something is missing from the song's story. Right now it's about a woman who leaves her family for a new life, but that isn't resonating with me. I crave more connection. Maybe it needs a long keyboard solo like Tori put in "Icicle."

Jack and Mariah come down the stairs, laughing about some inside joke. "Tad can't make it," Jack says offhandedly. "Just the three of us tonight."

"Oh, yeah? Maybe we should have rehearsed at the meeting the other day."

He sighs and reaches for the guitar he wants, hung up next to the others along the back wall. "Don't tell me you're bent out of shape about that, Florence."

"Using my name? Wow, we went from neutral to annoyed fast." I lay down a few more chords. "We don't have to rehearse. The two of you can do what you want."

"I don't think we can afford to do that." Jack's voice is dark and husky as if the stakes are too great for them to miss it. "We need to be tight for Beachland. And then we'll need to rehearse for the PTA thing."

I roll my eyes. "Why didn't you tell me we were doing that?"

"I never volunteered." Jack rolls his eyes back. "I was voluntold."

"Barlow is my alma mater," Mariah says. "I told Patricia I wanted to do this. It's very important to me. And this band doesn't belong to just the two of you."

We both gawk.

"Alright," I say. "Get out the setlist for the Beachland. We'll see if we can transfer some of that to the PTA gig."

After rehearsal, I can't get packed up fast enough, but Mariah darts in to stop me before I leave. "I'm sorry, I should have told you about the gig earlier."

"Three-way parenting is hard," I deadpan.

"Trust me, Florence, I know it's not about me." She waves her hands, and I catch sight of the ring. Shit, it is beautiful. A rose gold band with an understated marquis diamond in its center.

I shoulder my bag. "It sounds like it is, though."

I RELAY this story to Briar when she comes to pick up her kids Saturday night.

Grace and Aria are in first grade, identical, and a joy to be around. They'd spent most of the evening coloring and playing games with Teagan. Mellie isn't interested in babysitting, but Teagan had taken to the little girls easily. The three of them seem happy, so I invite Briar to come in and have a drink with me.

The two of us sit at the dining table with our glasses of white wine. Briar frowns. "She sounds like an idiot."

"Yeah... it's already the Mariah show and they haven't even gotten married." I take a long, cold sip. It feels good on my throat. "Jack just follows her around. And now I'm getting involved too."

"It's not just you." Briar's voice goes dark. "These women are manipulative. They're always shuffling around this or that responsibility. They act like they know everything, but they don't even do what they say they'll do. Someone else is always bailing them out, and I don't even know why."

I think back to Patricia, Annie, and their gorgeous crew. "Well, the more good-looking you are, the more hold you have on people."

"And they think they're so great because they always raise so much money every year. It's practically why Barlow is running. But this town is so richy-rich, and of course they want to support the kids at their school."

I lean back, crossing my arms with my wine hand close to my lips. "Do you think Mariah is involved with those women somehow?"

Briar's brow creased. "Why would you say that? She doesn't even have a kid in the school now."

"She will. When she marries Jack." Something flutters in my stomach when I say that. "Maybe that's why she felt brave enough to come out and say something to them."

She takes a sip. Her daughters are on the floor, heads bent with Teagan's over a Junie. B. Jones book. "I don't know. None of this adds up, Florence. The invitation, the voluntelling. The way they all seem so happy all the time."

I glance back at the trifecta of girls. "I guess some people are happy all the time?"

Briar follows my gaze. "Not possible."

WE HAVE STARTED ARGUING over who is going to play which new song at the PTA concert.

Jack wants to play the thing he wrote for Mariah. I want to play mine, which is coming along better and better. The woman in my song has now decided to stay instead of run, coming up against impossible odds. It's very Decemberists. "Why not both?" Tad asks helplessly, but he is ignored as the two of us snipe at each other.

Jack argues that since Mariah went to the Barlow School, she should be allowed to do more. But aside from the few and far between bass solos, there isn't much for a bass player to do besides keep the beat. "Why don't you liaise with the PTA women?" I suggest to Mariah. "I don't understand them and I never will. If you're from there—maybe you'd have a better rapport."

"What does that have to do with the set list?" Jack argues, but Mariah nods.

"I can see that," she tells me. "I did make this happen."

THE DAY of the fundraiser arrives. I've barely spoken to the PTA ladies this whole time, but Mariah has done a bang-up job. I suppose she does serve a function in our little broken-up family.

I have on my Florence makeup, a throwback to my early days when goth was in. It doesn't seem to have gone out, actually. I have on ripped denim shorts over leather leggings and a Metallica T-shirt. I'm ready to get this over with and on with my life.

The gym is filled with donors. There are so many more people here than I've ever seen in this space. People are in gala wear, long sparkly dresses and sequins, tuxedos. I'm glad the dress code doesn't apply to us. I slip my sound controller into my ear, and we're ready to go.

There's applause as we take the stage. Barlow does have a gorgeous auditorium, but there isn't room for donors to enjoy the fancy catering, so this is a makeshift temporary podium. I've sung at huge venues. This is high school. Literally.

I catch sight of Briar. She's hard to find, sitting at one of the back tables in a plain black dress. She's wearing makeup, though, and her face is bright. I don't feel so alone.

Everyone is eating while we play. I'm hoping I can snag a plate before we go—it looks good. At least my peckishness distracts me while Jack performs his solo song. I wish mine was ready.

When we're done, there is enthusiastic applause. I'm about to get up when Patricia Richards climbs to the lectern. "Let's thank Save the Kids for their amazing performance!" she yells, and the crowd sends up another roar. It does kind of feel nice, I think. People who would never know that Jack and I used to be together were listening.

"Before we start the main part of the program, I'd like to invite another musical guest. If you've been here before, you know what I mean." Patricia winks at the crowd, and more applause ripples from the tables. I have not been here before, so I do not know what they mean. My ears are still ringing from our set, and I adjust my earplug. Too much sound damage from our early days.

A group of PTA women files onto the stage in front of us. "Please welcome to Barlow's own *a cappella* group," Patricia says. She sidles away from the lectern and into the line with Annie Vane and the others. I suddenly feel stupid in my goth makeup and look out at Briar. Her back is straight as she waits patiently for them to start.

I blink as Mariah sets her bass on her stand and strides up to the front. She takes a place in the center of the eight women. *Of course,* I think. Two on a part. I crane my neck backward to meet Jack's eyes, and he shrugs.

They start singing.

Dread pools in my belly. This is a new feeling, something I don't understand. I'm unsettled. Their song isn't the sweet crooning I expected. It's unholy, unreal, chords moving between tonal and atonal and not finding any resolution.

What's scarier are the looks on the donors' faces. Their expressions have all flattened, their faces slack. My stomach turns as I inspect each one of them, each a drone in a collective. Not one of them is moving. Not even my friend, whose body is now relaxed, her gaze locked on the stage.

I'm shaking, and I want to sit down, but there's only my stool behind the keyboard. So I perch on it and watch the women. They extend their hands to each other and then they fucking *levitate.* All in one giant pod. Mariah is enraptured. Each one of them has that long hair flying out behind them, their perfect highlights splayed in the air.

I will it to end, but it doesn't stop. Not until all the donors have sunk off their chairs onto the floor. Some people are twitching. There's a man in the very front who looks like he survived the Civil War, and I fear for his back breaking. So many fragile people.

Then, finally, the women float to the ground. The crashing in my belly turns to a fizzy lightness, still fearful but full of new adrenaline.

I pat the squishy earplug I'd kept in. I'm afraid to take it out.

THEY'VE SET ASIDE a table with plates and drinks for us, but I can't eat. Can't even sip champagne. Mariah is holding court, preening as guests and PTA members approach her. They lavish her with praise, raving about her talent. Jack and I hunch over untouched salads, and I wonder if he's going to bring it up. I don't see Tad anywhere.

Patricia Richards comes up to us before anyone else does. She touches my shoulder, and I flinch, but she doesn't blink. "What did you think of our song?" she asks.

"Very good," Jack says curtly as he plays with his fork.

"Unconventional," I say. "Who composed that? Schoenberg?"

Her expression is blank. "I'm not familiar."

"Felt very twelve-tone," I continued. "Someone in your group knows their stuff."

Patricia rearranges her face into a wide smile. "We do sound nice, don't we? Now, I wondered if you had a check for us."

"How long has your group been around?" I turn to my side at the sound of Jack's baritone.

"Oh, for decades." She waves a hand. I catch sight of her latest manicure, a pure white gel painted with a silver pattern. I wonder what her husband does that she can afford that style. But then, I suppose she could always sing for it.

"Let us know when you can stop by the donation table," she continues. "We take credit. For a small fee, of course."

When she's gone, I check that Mariah isn't listening, then lean
toward my ex. "What the fuck was that?"

His eyes go wide, and he points to the donation table. People are
lined up in droves to hand over their checks and credit cards—for a
small fee, of course—to Annie Vane and company. They're so grateful,
accepting the money with huge smiles and hands pressed together to
show their great thanks.

"They made them donate," Jack says softly.

"Did you know she could do that kind of thing? Mariah, I mean."

Jack and I were together so long. Since we were children, basically. I
can read any twitch of his eye, any quirk of his mouth. He didn't know. I
can tell even before he shakes his head.

IT TAKES us an hour or so to get all the equipment together and loaded.
Tad is wrecked. His long hair is stringy, his skin shimmering with sweat.
I take the extra time to help him move his gear when I'm done with
mine. Jack and Mariah take off in the van before we do—they have all
the supplementary items since our rigs are bigger. I hitch up the trailer
and drive the truck over to Jack and Mariah's place.

"You okay?" I ask Tad as I navigate the short ride.

He shakes his head. "I don't feel well."

Tad has been sober for several years now. I wouldn't think he'd
break that for a gig at a private school, but now that I've seen the way
these women operate, anything is possible. I shiver at the thought.

"I didn't have any champagne," he offers.

"Of course not." I feel a flash of shame that I even considered it.
"What's wrong, then?"

"After the set. That whole thing. None of it made any sense."

"God." We stop at a red light, and I scrub a hand over my face. "I'm
still shaken."

"That song... it was so beautiful."

The light changes. I grip the wheel tighter.

"It was… I've never heard anything like that. I felt like I was floating. Flying. Something changed in me," he continues. "Maybe I'm coming down from that."

I feel cold as I pull carefully into their driveway. "Tad, did you have your earplugs in when they started singing?"

When I open the door, the cab light flicks on. Tad's face is drawn, pale. He moves his head just slightly. Enough for me to worry.

I jump out and hit the button to open the garage. I'm about to go inside when I hear them.

My heart pounds. Tad isn't okay. He needs water. He needs to lie down. But they are yelling so loud.

"How many times, Mariah?" Jack is roaring. I clench my eyes shut and tamp down the emotions rising to the surface. *How many times did you scream at me like that?*

She's not giving it back. She's whimpering. "I can't even tell you, okay?"

"You can't tell me because you don't want to? Or because you don't even know?"

"I don't know, okay?" she wails.

Jack's voice grows cold. The sign he's serious, the sign his rage has burned off and that stoic, dangerous anger has set in. "You're a liar. Get out."

Mariah comes tearing out, her long hair flying past me.

"Hey!" I yell. "You can't leave."

She turns around, teeth bared. "I can do whatever I want."

"Please. I need your help. Tad's sick."

Her shoulders slump. She takes a few steps forward. I can see the exhaustion weighing her down. "That happens sometimes," she says.

"Is it serious? He looks horrible."

Mariah takes a deep breath, then rounds the back of the trailer to meet Tad at the passenger side. I'm about to follow when she hisses at me like an animal. I take the hint and get out of the way. God, I hope she's not stealing his soul or something.

I imagine Jack inside, balling his fists, teeth clenched together. I hope he doesn't put a hole into a wall. It's happened before.

It feels like an eternity when Mariah steps away. She's changed somehow. Her skin is green, sallow. Her hair looks papery thin, a world away from the sleek, perfumed style it had not even a minute before. She's even moving strangely. She's jerky, disjointed.

"He'll be okay now," she says, monotone.

"What about you?" I step toward her. This is probably the most empathy I've felt for her... maybe ever. "You don't look good."

"Duh." She sneers. "I gotta go."

I want to ask her a million questions, like what even the fuck is she? Where did she come from? What did she do to Tad? I hear Jack's voice echoing: *How many times?*

She doesn't even get in her car. I watch her walk away, her body stiff under the suburban streetlamps.

I slide back around the cab and assess Tad. He's sitting forward now, leaning on his knees, breathing hard. When he moves his hands from his face, I see that his skin is pinking up. He blinks a few times as if to make sure he knows who he's talking to. "That was fucked up, Florence."

"Yeah." I blow out a breath. "I'm glad you're okay."

I install Tad on our—*their*—living room couch and come back out to help Jack unload. It's harder work with only the two of us. I smell the sweat on him. My makeup is melting onto my face. We don't speak. I don't think either one of us wants to relive this night.

We come to the unspoken agreement of leaving the trailer hitched. I grab my purse out of the truck and hitch it onto my shoulder. I'd thought Jack would go back inside, but he's waiting there. He looks like a little boy who's lost his favorite toy.

"You think you can take care of Tad?" I motion to the house. "He's doing better, but..."

I don't want to explain to Jack what happened. I don't think I can.

"He's not…"

"He's sober. Just a bellyache, I think."

"Oh, thank God." Jack spins in a circle, hand in his hair. "God, Florence."

It's a reflex move, born from years unable to see him cry. I slide up against him and wrap him into a hug. Lean my head into his chest, close my eyes, pretend.

He squeezes me hard. We stay like that for a few minutes, until he moves away and dips down to kiss me. Another reflex. I relax into the feel of his pillowy lips, his hands tight against my waist.

Then I gasp, pull away.

His eyes are glazed, half-lidded. "What?"

"I have to get the girls."

"Get them. Come back here." He wraps his arms around me again. "Please. I don't want to be alone."

"Tad will be with you. He can sleep in the guest room. I'll call you in the morning, okay?"

I squeeze him one more time. My heart is speeding—not just from kissing him. It's picked up some extra beats for Briar.

I PULL up to the curb in front of Briar's house and run to her door.

She sees me on the Ring camera and ushers me inside. I study her for any signs of illness and let out a deep breath when I realize she looks okay. Her face is scrubbed clean of makeup, her hair springy from a wash.

"What's wrong? Do you want some coffee?" Briar's brow is creased in concern as she leads me into the living room. Her girls are asleep on the couch, and mine are buried in their phones.

I shake my head. "I just wanted to make sure you were okay."

"Why wouldn't I be? You told me you would be late back."

"No, I mean… after the thing at the school."

I know she was taken in. I could see it on her face. I saw her at the donation table. Briar can't afford to give tons of money. How much had they taken her for? I'll Venmo her later. Come up with some stupid reason.

"Why wouldn't I be okay?"

I fumble over my words, but the lie that comes out does seem convincing, even to me. "Our drummer got sick. I was worried food poisoning might be going around."

Briar nods. "Oh, that's sweet. Thank you so much for checking on me. I'm totally fine."

It's going on midnight by now, and the girls are straggling to their feet. I can text Briar in the morning. So why don't I want to leave?

Because I don't know what switches have been pulled inside of her. Because I don't know if my new friend is who she used to be. Has everything about her been changed by only a few minutes of song?

~

JACK DOESN'T SAY anything to me when we swap the kids the next day. Mariah isn't there, and I don't ask. Instead, I stop for an iced chai and then retire to my studio, where I work on my song for hours until I disappear into it.

That evening, I grab a salad from Panera and read on my phone in the café. I'm going down a rabbit hole of monsters and science fiction trying to figure out what these women are. Stepford Wives are the obvious possibility, but can robots levitate like that? Besides, Jack would have known. Maybe, if he wasn't so far up his own ass.

It's not that I don't believe I kissed him last night. I know exactly why I did. I also know why I stopped. Not just because of Briar, not just because of the girls, but because it would have shattered more glass. Sent shards flying.

I halt my scrolling at a vague recollection of high school mythology. Odysseus, lashing himself to a ship mast because he didn't want to be taken in by singing sirens. I comb through the Wikipedia article. Don't have to be a rocket scientist to know I'm right.

There's some chattering going on in a corner. I only notice it when I come out of my screen-induced reverie. It's the women from the PTA

—I recognize Patricia and Annie. Some of the other familiar faces from their little concert. I scan the group for Mariah, but she isn't there.

Then my gaze rests on Briar.

She looks like them. Glossy lips, perfectly lined eyes. Chic in a camel jacket and luxe black pants. Her shiny red hair is straight as a pin.

I go home. I'm totally alone apart from Fiona—the only sounds in the house are the soft thumps of her skulking around. I hate this time of night. I can't sleep, I don't want to watch TV, and I'm too exhausted to start anything new. So I go into the studio and play through the song a couple times.

I feel like it's ready. This is a new thought, formed somewhere between when I left for Panera and when I got home. There's no true knowledge of when a creative project is complete; I can always tinker with it even more. But if I don't stop, don't let it breathe and rest, I will over-edit, overthink the entire thing. I have to let it be what it is.

It's me. It's Florence. It's not Save the Kids, it's not A Particular Melancholy, it's not me and Jack. It's me, and I don't belong to anyone.

A hundred ideas swirl in my head, but the prevailing one reaches in and grabs me by the throat. Maybe it's selfish, maybe it's a plea for attention. I don't care.

I record the song and post it on our social media.

My dreams are wild. The music world worships me like they used to. Like when I sang for Phillip the Masked the first time. When I first felt that adoration from the crowd, carrying me somewhere into the stratosphere. I see Tad, hear the wonder in his voice as he tells me he floated for the first time. There's a man knocking at my door, and when I throw it open he smiles and tells me how much he loved it and how he wants to take me to dinner. I feel like I'm dropping through time, falling through clouds.

I wake up, blink my eyes open, and scrabble for my phone on the bed next to me. I sit up and arrange myself on the pillows, clutching it hard.

The song doesn't have any comments yet. I check all the places I've posted it, but no one has seen it. I know if I went through our admin dashboard, I could see how many views it's gotten, even how many listens from our hosted audio server. But I don't want to. Maybe it'll take a little longer for the world to be awed by me.

I do have a text from Jack. *Saw your post.*

Yeah? I tap back.

He replies right away. *Good song.*

Thanks.

You want to play it at the next rehearsal?

I stop and lick my lips. *Uh, sure?*

It really is great, Florence.

I don't know what to type back, so I don't. Besides, the little dots below the text are waving. I wait.

I think we should take the kids out of Barlow.

Duh, I think, channeling my inner Mariah. But I am more polite as I reply that I agree.

GRASSMAN

He was too young for love. But the moment he saw her, that flashing light, it felt like time stopped. He couldn't resist.

He left the woods. Past the places where the smooth-skinned people lived. He'd caught the two females watching him. Several times, and always at night. They gaped at him, and he wondered what made him so fascinating. He was just a boy, living his life like any other grassman.

True, it was unlike him to leave the woods. The terrain turned to an odd texture beneath his feet. Gritty and hard. Black, blacker than the soil and dirt he was used to. And a certain kind of dusty.

Lights sped by. He'd seen them before, careening through the dark, but he had never been this far up close. These weren't just lights. They made sounds: roaring, whooshing. They were powerful entities, and he needed to be careful.

She was shining, so close. Her head tapered into a crown, and her body flared out from that. And her skin was so bright, the only color in such a dark world. Orange ringed with silver. She was a beacon.

He reached out to her, pulled her in close. She felt different, too. Smooth. But resistant in some places as he ran his hand over her body. Pliant, but pushing back.

There were others like her, spooling out into a row, one behind another on the road. But he didn't need them. She had caught his eye first.

He lifted her easily and held her over his back. He loved the feel of that texture against his fringe. She didn't speak, but he didn't either. They'd find other ways to express themselves.

He couldn't admit it to himself, but he was lonely. He thought of those creatures, those *girls*, with their messy hair and staring eyes. They could not be his friends. They both frightened and irritated him. They treated him like a freak; they goggled at the sight of him. He wasn't a show for them to watch. He had his own life to live, and they weren't the companions he wanted.

She, however—his new soulmate, the one who shone a light into him and hit him in his tender spots—she accepted him as he was. She submitted to him and he took her willingly.

He carried her back to his burrow and crawled inside. He placed her in the middle of the small cave and wrapped his body around her until the sun came up.

EVEN HISTORY BURNS

The man I didn't know squinted at me from across the table.

"Even if what you're saying is true," he said, pointing a fork at me, "there's no way a python could have done that."

I looked past him at the historic building behind the window. We were at the Winking Lizard, a local haunt with free popcorn and bar food. Behind him, I could see the wreckage of the historic bike shop. A shame.

I'd met this man—Ross—on an over-fifty dating app, Carpe Diem. Apparently when you are over fifty, you must seize the day because you don't have that many days left. My friend Laurie had turned me on to it. She'd never been married but found love and a husband on the app. While we sat at this very bar one night, she grabbed my arm and squeezed it. "Deb, I never thought this would happen," Laurie said, her yellow hair haloed in neon light. "You have to try it."

"It's a menace," I told Ross as I picked up a mozzarella stick. I didn't even care if I got oil on my chin. At fifty-five, I had no fucks left to give. "It'll try anything. And I'd say this is the worst thing it's ever done."

I couldn't tell how old Ross was. He still had hair, though it was thin and sparse. The usual wrinkles: crow's feet, the beginnings of jowls. I was too familiar with those signs of aging. My own hair, which used to be so lush and thick, had dwindled to a fine, stringy mess. Ross had that typical engineer look—wire-rimmed glasses and a collared plaid shirt.

"Do you know how the fire started?" he asked.

I shook my head. "All the more reason to suspect it."

He pulled out his phone, and his thumbs started flying. I bristled and picked up another cheese stick. I hate it when people google after I've told them something. Like they don't believe me. Have to confirm it for themselves.

Ross was my first date from this app. I'd been divorced for ten years by this point, and I'd sworn I'd never date again. Being alone was fine. I didn't feel like I was missing something. Yet there was some jealousy, some feeling like I'd wasted my time. I lived in a sexless marriage for so many years, and I wondered if that part of me—the passionate, romantic part—could reawaken.

I watched him type and told myself I was being unrealistic about getting together with my first Carpe Diem date. *You have to kiss a lot of frogs.*

He looked up, blinked at me from behind those round glasses. "Huh. Interesting."

The server came and cleared the empty appetizer plate. We both ordered burgers. An easy meal. We'd get done about the same time, ask for the check, and split it down the middle. Ross and I had chatted for a few weeks, and I hadn't felt much of a spark. I'd hoped things would be different when we met in person, but I was disappointed. My daughter would be, too. She was waiting at home for my report.

I didn't want to deal with awkward silences, though. Or awkward conversations. I was determined to at least carry on a dialogue with this man. "What'd you find?" I asked.

"It says they don't know what caused the fire."

That's what I just told you, genius. "Uh-huh."

"And snakes can't really cause fires."

I lifted my chin. "Okay."

He took a sip of his beer. I mirrored him with my pink Cosmo.

"Are you being serious with me?" Ross leaned in. "You don't actually believe in all this, do you?"

I smirked. "What do you think?"

WE ATE OUR BURGERS. I expected that to be the end of it until he reached for the check.

I clucked and tried to grab it. "We can split. It's okay."

Ross pulled the check back toward his chest, as if he were protecting it. "No. I invited you out."

"But aren't we..."

He narrowed his eyes. "Aren't we what?"

"I don't know," I blubbered.

He opened the leather sleeve and scribbled his name. I craned my neck to see what kind of tip he left. A generous one. Good man. "You're saying you don't want to see me again, aren't you?"

My skin was on fire. I was sure I was tomato-red. "It depends. Do you want to see me again?"

Ross left the folded sleeve at the end of the table and blinked at me. He was most definitely owlish. "I find you interesting, even if there is no attraction between us."

It was my turn to blink—I was, to be honest, offended. "Is there? We haven't discussed attraction."

"Let's go." He motioned to the door. "Walk and talk."

PENINSULA IS best when it's warm. People mill about the town, riding bikes, walking on the towpath trail. Enjoying the water flowing below the bridge. The Cuyahoga Valley train comes trundling along, and passengers wave from the windows. I welcomed the wind that picked up my hair and wafted it around my shoulders.

Even though it was getting dark, I followed Ross down the path next to the railroad tracks, across from the rubble of the old store. I could have begged out—after all, he'd said there was no spark. But I was curious about where he was taking this.

"So it was an escaped circus animal," he lectured as we started walking. "Not much to write home about."

I'd grown up hearing about the creature. Any mischief or concern in town could be explained by the snake's meddling. I'd always found it funny that the huge, bulky creature could be the cause of so much angst. And did I actually believe it? Probably not. But the fact that this guy was questioning me got under my skin.

"It's not supposed to be here, though." I jogged a little to keep up with him. He wasn't too tall, but he had long legs, and I was short. "It doesn't belong."

"Seems like a mistake that it was dropped here, though. There aren't pythons in Northeast Ohio."

"Of course it was a mistake." I gritted my teeth. "And I can guarantee it doesn't want to be here."

I heard him smack his lips. "Do pythons even live that long? This article says the circus happened in 1944."

"This one does. I don't know what else to tell you, man."

He stopped and turned around to face me. I came to an abrupt halt. We pressed into each other for a moment before parting.

"I suppose it's not about the python," he mused. "I'm fascinated that you continue to insist this legend is true."

Ross lived in Independence, not too far from here. Carpe Diem can cast a wide net, but I'd limited the search. I didn't want to drive an hour if a relationship worked out. Maybe I was planning ahead too far. How long until I exhausted all the possibilities? When there were no good single men left within a fifteen-mile triangulation of me? My demographic was divorced guys and widowers. It was slim pickings.

"We haven't talked about much else," I said. "Where are you from?"

"Michigan," he said. "Yes, the home of Bigfoot. Which I also don't believe in."

"There's the Cuyahoga Valley Grassman here too. A cousin of Bigfoot, I believe. You might find some roaming in the park."

Ross grumbled.

"I'm serious. Tell me about how you grew up." I hustled to keep up with him. "My mother was pretty woo-woo. She always wanted us to look past the obvious. To see what might be lurking beyond what's right in front of us."

"Who's *us*?"

"My sister and me." I thought back to my mother with a pang in my chest. To the sister who'd betrayed me in the worst possible way. "I'm asking about you, though."

He shrugged. "A little boring life. Only child. My parents were older, never wanted kids. I was bookish, shy."

"You've never been married?"

He shook his head but didn't elaborate.

I took a second to listen and think. It was nearly full dark, and the forest around us closed in with deeper shadows. The crickets and peepers filled the air with an eerie song. The soil surrounding the pavement was loamy, pungent. The traffic had slowed down.

It suddenly occurred to me that Ross might be trying to kill me.

I pulled in a gasp.

"What?"

I could barely see him now. "Are you a serial killer?"

"What?" Ross turned back, and I bumped into him again. This time, my skin brushed against his.

Maybe he was wrong. Maybe there was a tiny spark. If he wasn't a serial killer. There was still the good possibility of that.

"Why are we all the way out here?"

He sighed. "I suppose we should turn back around. I can use the flashlight on my phone."

I whipped my phone out and turned mine on too. The path lit up with an eerie glow.

Now we were side by side, moving at the same pace.

"So do you want to see me again?" I asked. The date was almost over. I might as well be up front about it.

Ross was silent. Sounded like a no, like he was thinking about letting me down gently. That was fine, really. I'd been chatting with a few other guys. I could set up a few more dates. I was doing this for fun, right?

Was I even having fun right now? It was kind of cool out here. Not just figuratively—the air had cooled too as the sun went down. A sense of peace hovered around us along with the fear that lived in the dark.

"Is the python out here?" he asked.

"That is not an answer."

"I want to see this so-called mysterious snake." He paused. "Think of how you'd be celebrated if you found the cause of the fire. I googled. If there was a heat lamp in the back of the shop, it could malfunction and start a pretty angry fire."

"That would mean someone was taking care of it. Providing it with heat."

"And it doesn't have anywhere else to go," Ross said. "Might be around here."

WE RETURNED to the town proper. Streetlights bathed the sidewalks. I didn't realize how tight my chest had been until I relaxed. He could go to his car, I could go to mine, and we'd be done with all of it.

But instead of moving onto the bridge, Ross hesitated at the site of the fire. He started picking his way into the rubble.

"What are you doing?" My voice cracked with shock. "That's a historic building. They're going to try and restore it."

"Too late now." He headed to where the back of the building had been. "A snake lamp would be metal, right? It wouldn't have burned with the rest."

I threw up my hands. "I don't know! Why do you have to be so scientific about everything?"

"I'm a scientific person. That's how I operate. Logic and facts." He shined his flashlight down. "And the evidence isn't looking good."

I folded my arms. "Facts aren't everything."

"Most things can be explained with logic."

I thought about Wendy and me. How we would leave the house at night, just like this, and hunt in the woods. Trying to sneak a glimpse of the Grassman or the Python just to say we witnessed them. Something to take back to the kids at school. Something to be proud of. A sighting that would prove the creatures' existence, that would make everyone jealous. How ironic.

"My husband cheated on me with my sister," I blurted out.

Ross looked up. His face was half lit. He pointed at the ground. "Snake lamp," he said.

AND THAT WAS how I found myself huddling under a tree and waiting for the Python to arrive.

It was warm, even a little humid, and Ross's body next to me felt like a heater. We needed to save our battery, so Ross held his flashlight out while I kept mine tucked away in my pocket.

He'd said I might have told the truth but that he needed more evidence.

I'd already told Ross logic didn't count for anything. That Wendy and I had seen that long, fat tail moving through the woods in the dark. Our mother, single, piecing that house together so we'd have a safe place to sleep and food on our table. All the things she did to make us happy. And she didn't even know about Wendy, about what I had lost. "We never meant to do it," she'd said. "It just happened."

"How long do you intend to sit here?" I asked Ross.

He had begun to sweat, and I could smell it on his skin, mixing with whatever Old Spice deodorant or body spray he had on. "Until we figure out what we're doing," he said.

"Isn't it like three in the morning by now?"

"Shhhh," he said. I grumbled in response.

I'm too old for this, I thought. I inched backwards to rest against a tree. Every part of me ached. I closed my eyes, and stars brightened against the screen inside my mind.

"Deb!"

I blinked awake, and my back screamed. "Huh?"

Ross lowered his voice to a whisper. "C'mon. Quiet."

Though I tired of his orders, I crept back to where he was standing. How was he still on his feet? I made a note to renew my gym membership.

He pointed. I squinted into the dark. There was movement, but it was so dark with Ross's flashlight off. Besides the moonlight, maybe a stray streetlamp was providing ambient illumination.

Was that it? A slight swaying in the dark. A long, fat tail, slicing through the grass.

Ross swore and turned off his flashlight.

"I need to go home," I said.

It was noon by the time I woke up the next morning. My eyes were bleary as I wandered into the kitchen and searched for a coffee pod. I found my phone blown up with calls and texts from my daughter.

"Where are you?" she shrieked into my voicemail. That was how you knew things were serious: a millennial made a phone call and even left a message.

I leaned against my kitchen counter and sighed, then called back as my single-serve machine burbled.

Stevie answered. "Thank God! I was worried sick."

"Clearly." I scrubbed a hand over my face. "Are you better now?"

"I will be." She let out a long breath. "So tell me about it."

I gave her the brief story. She didn't interrupt, but when I got to the end, she began to guffaw. I could picture her in her little Cleveland Heights apartment, cross-legged on the aged carpet, hooting.

"Mom. You're too much." She paused. "Are you going to see him again?"

"I don't know." I crossed the kitchen to get my cup out of the machine. The sun shone through my lacy curtains. Outside my condo, people were out and about, getting their vitamin D. "The whole thing was kind of weird."

"I'd say." Stevie's voice went small. "And the whole thing with Aunt Wendy."

I went still. I knew Stevie had contact with them—he was her dad, after all, and we'd shared custody for the few years she'd still been a minor. But I'd diligently avoided my sister since the confession that destroyed me. It hadn't destroyed my life—I was doing fine on my own—but I'd been torn up ever since.

"Yeah," I said.

"Do you miss her?"

"I guess I do." I recovered enough to take a sip of my coffee. It was already cool. That machine couldn't make a hot cup to save its life. "That ship has sailed, though."

"You don't even want to tell her what you saw? Or supposedly saw?"

"No," I said sharply.

Stevie was quiet. I heard scuffling in the background. Her cat? A boyfriend? Suddenly I felt far away from her. From all of it.

"What if I tell her I talked to you?"

I blinked. I would not cry. "I can't stop you from doing that. You're your own person."

"Okay," Stevie said. "Well, text me."

I downed the rest of the coffee. "Yeah."

THE AFTERNOON LED to the usual Saturday activities. Laundry, reading, nap. Once I dug myself out of my sleepy hole, I turned on the TV and watched old game shows while I ate leftover Mongolian beef from Thursday. It was a good recipe, and easy. One of my regulars in rotation.

I was about to run the bath when my phone chirped. A text from "Ross Tech Guy" popped into my message list.

Hey

That's it? A "hey" without even punctuation?

Hey is for horses, I typed back.

He sent back a tongue-sticking-out emoji. *Sorry. I'm not good at this. This what?*

Talking to women.

I turned off the water and sat on the toilet lid. *Good thing I'm not just a woman.*

He didn't reply right away. I channeled my daughter's hearty laugh. He probably thought I was an alien or something. I got up and started running the water again, watched it steam up.

The phone dinged again. I imagined him carefully typing: *What does that mean?*

I'm a python hunter.

Another tongue sticking out emoji. I laughed again and turned off the water once more. *So did you get enough evidence?*

I need more, actually. Want to go back out next week?

I was still smiling when I finally got into the tub.

I lay back, the steam wafting over me. It felt good on my sore muscles, and I sank deeper into the water. I closed my eyes and let the screen inside my mind go blank.

Somewhere in there, I saw Wendy. Her bare feet on soiled ground. Her cherry-print pajamas, the smell of baby shampoo in her long, stringy hair. Her mischievous grin. My stomach soured, but I was rooted to my spot, the hot water eddying around me. I heard her laugh, like she was dead, only a memory.

As I watched, her body turned to smoke. All at once, like she was collapsing into a thousand tiny puffs. Behind her, a long, fat tail swayed.

BEES AND LEMONS

Most days, Katrin's pain was bearable. She'd sit outside on the back deck with a cup of tea, watching the river flow by, admiring the animals that came and went. Sometimes there were deer—they'd creep from the woods adjoining the property, timid at first but then bold, sometimes coming all the way up to Katrin. She was high above them, so they must have felt safe. They grunted in greeting, and they sounded like horses.

Her husband was not usually home. He was saving his PTO. But if it was a nice day, she'd sit outside long into the night. Walter would come home from work and click his teeth at her while stepping delicately onto the wood planks. "You'd better be careful out here. We really need to replace it... I don't want you to fall through."

She'd blink at him. "Does it matter at this point?"

Since they stopped the chemo, Katrin had struggled to accept the next phase of her life. The ending of it. Her mind fought the cancer as her body threatened to break down. Eventually, the body would win. And so Katrin needed to be outside. She needed as much sun as she could get. Perhaps her death would come in winter.

She still liked to read. Audiobooks were a pleasure, actors' voices streaming into the air, weaving stories. Other times she'd choose music, and not the soothing bullshit dying people were supposed to like. Katrin liked metal, hard rock, the kind of songs that protested the ordinary. She let her rage blast out one playlist at a time.

Katrin was listening to Korn when she spotted the beekeeper crossing through their shared yard. She tapped her phone to stop the music and tottered to her feet.

The beekeeper held up a hand. "None of that. I'm coming to you."

"The stairs are flimsy," Katrin said, but her voice could no longer come out loud enough for a yell. "Be careful."

"Oh, I always am." The woman took a seat in a deck chair across from Katrin's outdoor couch.

The beekeeper, despite her advanced age, always looked radiant. She glowed with some kind of ethereal light. Katrin's chest flared with jealousy. She'd never been this close to the woman, and seeing her up close reminded Katrin how much of life she would miss when she died.

Katrin rearranged her features into a smile. "What can I help you with?"

"This isn't a transaction, dear." The beekeeper held up a hand. "I saw you and wanted to say hello."

They'd only ever talked in passing. Katrin reasoned that the woman was curious about Katrin's illness. The beekeeper had probably seen Katrin's hair fall out, had observed that she no longer went to work each day. Maybe she saw Katrin outside. Katrin saw her, after all, as she tended to her hives.

"Well, hello," Katrin said. She waited for the woman to ask how she felt.

"I'm Cleo. It's nice to meet you." Cleo reached across the porch and held out her hand. Katrin shook it and introduced herself too.

They sat there for a few empty moments while Katrin tried to think up something to say. Her brain wasn't all where it used to be.

"I should have introduced myself a long time ago," Cleo said finally. She gestured to the big backyard. "We've been sharing the same space for so long."

Katrin and Walter had lived there seven years. They'd spent most of those trying to have a baby. *Tragedy after tragedy,* she imagined the neighbors saying. *So unlucky. Wonder if the husband will marry again. Have a kid with the new wife.*

Walter had never made Katrin feel replaceable, but she knew she was. Her job was posted only two days after her resignation.

Katrin managed a smile. "I'm sure you've heard all about me."

Cleo shifted, shook her head. "I don't talk much to anyone."

Maybe the woman wasn't here for gossip. But Katrin was tired. She needed to go inside. "I have to excuse myself," she said. Cleo got up and helped Katrin to her feet.

She wasn't eating much anymore. Katrin's hospice nurse, Haley, had told her this would happen. Gently, of course. Everything Haley said was gentle. As if Katrin needed to be rocked like a baby into her night.

Haley came to the house at least once a day. Checked Katrin's vitals, had her rate her pain. Made sure she got some water and didn't need help using the toilet or taking a bath. Haley was a nice girl, Katrin thought, but she was just that—a girl. Haley didn't seem to understand the minutiae of death. Not that Katrin knew, either, but she'd read a lot of books.

When Katrin was newly engaged, she'd read so many books on weddings. She checked out bridal magazines from the library and pored through wedding organizers. She kept spreadsheets of invitations and thank-you notes. When they bought the house, she spent hours curating the perfect decorations and made a careful facilities plan for future repairs and upgrades. And when they wanted to have a baby, she kept an ovulation tracker. Checked her temperature every morning. Later, she took extensive notes on IVF and infertility. Grief after miscarriage. A book had never steered Katrin wrong.

Katrin knew what would happen. First, food wouldn't sound good to her anymore. She'd be down to applesauce and yogurt and then nothing at all. Then water would go. She might rally, but it wouldn't be for long. Someone from her past would visit her and beckon her to the other side. It would be a hallucination, but Katrin would think it was very real. She'd start to lose consciousness one moment at a time. Her breathing would go slow and shallow. Death rattling. Her hearing would be the last to go. She wanted Walter to talk to her like it was any other day. Tell her how work was going. What he ate for lunch.

KATRIN'S FEET could barely carry her. Haley helped her to the porch but cautioned that Katrin would need to be very careful coming back in. "I don't like this porch," she tutted. "You could hurt yourself."

Same thing she'd said to Walter. It didn't matter. Katrin didn't bother to say anything to Haley, though.

Cleo was outside, and Katrin waved to her. Cleo waved back. She wore her beekeeping outfit: head covering, gloves, white jacket. Her hives looked like layered stacked boxes, set up next to the trees at the back of the property line.

It wasn't long before Cleo came to the porch. "Hello, Katrin," she said as she climbed the stairs. "How's your day going?"

Katrin shrugged. "Same as always."

"The sun's nice. But the shade is too." Cleo sat in the same chair and pointed up at the tent that covered them.

"No doubt."

There still wasn't much to talk about. But Cleo tried. She asked Katrin to tell her about herself. It felt like a job interview. And she didn't have the energy for much exposition.

Cleo got up again. "Well. It's nice to see you, Katrin. Same time tomorrow?"

Katrin couldn't argue with that. She had no other plans.

KATRIN WOKE the next morning with a stomachache. Rain poured, soaking the trees outside their bedroom. Walter got her a glass of water and kissed her on the forehead. Haley would come later. She had a key. Katrin put an audiobook on her phone and drifted back off to sleep.

Katrin was just waking when the rain subsided and the sun came out. Haley came in for her usual routine, and Katrin asked if Haley could take her outside. Haley gave her a withering look. "With it being so slippery out there, I don't think it's a good idea."

"Please." Katrin couldn't keep the irritation out of her voice.

"Yes, yes, I know, it doesn't matter anyway." Haley frowned and opened the back door. "Come on. If you're going to be that way."

Stubborn Gen Z. Katrin harrumphed and shuffled outside.

She sat in her chair and was getting settled in when Haley stopped. "What?" Katrin asked.

"Did you have your porch worked on?"

Katrin followed Haley's eyes to the formerly wobbly plank. "No, unless Walter did and hasn't told me?"

Haley's smile went a little manic. She hopped up and down, testing the waters at first, then full-on jumping. "It's fixed."

A lump formed in Katrin's throat. A reminder that the house would be standing even after she was gone.

She was back inside not long after that. She'd have to apologize to Cleo the next time they spoke. Katrin sat on the couch and watched *Jeopardy!* Although she couldn't remember any of the answers. Questions?

Walt came in some time later. He was dragging. Not sleeping. Katrin felt a pang knowing that this was all because of her. She was mourning for her own self, for the coming loss. And yet she wished for peace for Walt. That he would be free of her. Not her in particular—they loved each other fiercely—but of her illness. Their love would be a tangible thing, felt long after Katrin was gone, but the fact remained that she would be gone, and she was already halfway gone.

"Did you get the porch fixed?" she asked right away.

He set his keys down on the sideboard. "Huh?"

"That one wobbly plank. It's fixed."

Walt's brow furrowed. "I didn't do that."

"Haley jumped on it. She didn't fall through."

"Okay." He sounded irritated, and she flushed with regret. But he did go outside. She heard the back door bang, some scuffling, and then a return bang. *Hearing is the last to go.*

Katrin waited. She wouldn't prompt him or make him feel like she'd coerced him to go out there. Let him say what he wanted to say. And she wouldn't have to waste energy talking.

"You're right." Walt came back into the living room and slumped down on the couch beside her. "It's fixed."

"That's so odd," Katrin said.

"Yeah. It looked like someone caulked it with sap or something. Thick and goopy." He sighed. "Someone must have been a good Samaritan."

KATRIN AND CLEO met up whenever it was warm. They exchanged phone numbers. Katrin's hands were shaky as she typed hers into Cleo's. But Cleo texted, too—funny memes, usually, but sometimes emojis and stickers. Cleo didn't hold back with what she shared. She talked about her frustrations, her children, even her ex-husband. Katrin liked the easy conversation, a distraction from all she felt.

There was a cold snap one day in late August, and Cleo suggested Katrin come to her house. Katrin was weak and tired, but she was also curious. She wanted to see Cleo's place, and she reasoned she could sit on the couch just like she could at home. It was only down the street.

"Come in, come in!" Cleo threw open the door with gusto. Once Katrin was settled, Cleo brought her chamomile tea with lemon and honey courtesy of Cleo's bees.

Katrin couldn't say much. She sipped the tea while Cleo talked. After a while, Cleo stopped and fixed her eyes on Katrin. "It isn't much longer now," she said, not a question.

Katrin shook her head. There was nothing left in her body to even cry, so she sat with her head down.

"My dear, it's been so good getting to know you." Cleo reached over and patted Katrin's hand, and she felt a rush of electricity prick between the two of them. "I would be remiss if I didn't help you now."

"You fixed the porch," Katrin said. The tea mug was warm in her hands.

"You noticed that?" Cleo beamed as she sat back in the chair. "Well, that's only one of my superpowers."

Cleo brought Katrin to her feet. They went to the window, where they looked out over all the shared backyards: Katrin's, Cleo's, and the neighbor beside Cleo. Katrin could see the beehives clearly now, the brown boxes with their tiny round escape hatches. But there was also a tree she'd never noticed: a tall plant with round yellow fruit hanging from it.

Katrin blinked. "How do you have a lemon tree?"

"They're sensitive, but they can live here. That lemon in your tea is all-natural."

Katrin glanced back to the spot she'd left on the couch, where the tea sat on an end table.

"I must ask. How do you feel?"

Katrin stepped back to consider Cleo. The beekeeper had pulled her long gray hair into a messy ponytail. Her still-youthful face glowed. Her body was soft, curvy, a body that had lived well.

"I feel okay," Katrin said. "Why?"

"I think you should come over more often," Cleo said.

September came, and Katrin was still alive.

Her doctors marveled at her progress. "The tumors are shrinking," they reported. Katrin was eating again, gaining weight. It seemed like a miracle.

It wasn't even a question as to whether Cleo had facilitated Katrin's return to normal life. There was no other treatment besides Katrin's daily cups of tea with lemon and honey. And Cleo loved every second of it. On warmer days, she took Katrin outside and showed her how to care for the bees and the lemon tree. Katrin carefully noted the details: how to dress, how to use a smoker, how to reap the honey. She learned to keep the lemon tree warm and how to clean the area.

October came. November. Katrin marveled at every moment of her life. Her brain fog melted, and her mind came online. She did crossword puzzles. She read books made of paper. She drove to the library and the coffee shop.

It got dark earlier, and Katrin didn't see Cleo as much. How long, she thought, would her symptoms stay away if she wasn't drinking the tea? She began pounding on the door every morning, shivering in her parka and the knit hat that covered her short hair. But eventually, Cleo stopped answering.

She waited for relatives to clear out Cleo's house. She waited for her cancer to come back. So much for that reprieve. Katrin started reading more books about death, trying to prepare herself for the inevitable. She read books on grief as she tried to process her friend's death. She wondered if she was being too selfish about prolonging the miracle.

One night in December, Katrin couldn't sleep. She wandered around the house, aimless, sipping a tea that was nowhere near as powerful as Cleo's. She stared out the window. Who was taking care of the bees now? Where was the lemon tree?

Then Katrin noticed it. A warm light gathering around the bases of the hives. Like a sunbeam illuminating the dark. It got bigger, revolved further until it was a bubble in the air. Like a firework, it exploded, and Katrin gasped as the bubble expanded into the shape of a butterfly.

She was so tired, but she could barely sleep. She sat and stared at the backyard until dawn came. Frost blanketed the grass that bordered the sidewalk. She scurried up Cleo's porch steps and opened the storm door. There was a note taped to the main door, and Katrin ripped it away, gripping it with trembling hands.

I only have so much time here, Cleo had written in loopy script. *You have been my friend, and for that I am grateful. I don't know if I will come back, or if I can, but would you care for my bees and lemons?*

THE HOUSE WAS on the market for what felt like ten minutes. A young couple moved in, and Walter helped Katrin move the hives and the tree into their yard. "It's a shame," he said. "She was such a good friend to you."

"I miss her," Katrin said. There was a hole inside her where Cleo lived. Cleo, the butterfly, the light that filled the sky. "But I'll be okay."

Walt grinned and wiped sweat off his face with his covered shirt-sleeve. "I'm glad you've been going to book group, too."

"Yeah." She had to start small with making more friends. Katrin drank the special tea every night, but there was no telling when it might not work anymore. Every day was a roll of the dice. Only the rolls were coming up sixes so much more often.

KATRIN HAD JUST TURNED seventy-two when she got the news that the cancer had returned. Walt, too, had suffered: prostate cancer had taken him a few years back. It was just Katrin now. Their adopted daughter, Clara, was on a trip across Europe, although she assured Katrin she would be home as soon as she could.

The bees still lived in the backyard, but it was harder and harder to take care of them. She was getting tired again, that bone-weary ache, the knell that would eventually claim her.

It moved fast this time. Katrin chose not to pursue chemo. Clara came home and fussed over her; a new hospice nurse, Vanessa, came. Katrin wondered what had happened to Haley. It would have been too much of a coincidence if the same nurse had come years later.

She was outside tending to the bees when she saw a woman standing in Cleo's old yard. Katrin knew her—she and her husband had purchased the house shortly after Cleo moved on. The woman must have been in her twenties at the time. Now she looked older, even frail. When Katrin squinted, it looked like the woman's hair was a wig.

Katrin crossed the grass. "Hello," she said. "I should have introduced myself earlier. We've shared the same space for so long."

The woman blinked. Katrin knew how it felt. Being unable to speak. Being unable to form thoughts.

"I'm Katrin. I live in the house just right there." She pointed.

Her neighbor's face lit up. "Of course! You're the beekeeper. I'm May."

"May," Katrin said. "It's so good to meet you. You'll need to come over and try my tea. I use the honey from the bees and the lemons from the tree."

Katrin made tea for them both every day. It wasn't enough for her anymore, but it energized May. She got stronger with each cup, and Katrin's insides glowed. This was everything she'd ever wanted.

That last night, Katrin was alone in her house. After Katrin reassured her that everything would be okay, Clara went out with her friends from high school. Katrin settled herself at the kitchen table with a cup of tea and a notebook. She scribbled her final note to May and taped it to the door, mentally apologizing the whole time.

She wanted to be in the most comfortable place possible when she did it. So she climbed the stairs, carefully, until she reached their bed. She'd been sleeping downstairs in the hospital bed with the IVs and all that nonsense, but now she wanted to crawl back into the one she'd occupied for all those years. Even with fresh sheets, Katrin could smell the echoes of Walter, of them both. All those unexpected years.

Katrin closed her eyes. The world blanked out, and all she heard was a faded buzzing. A moment later, she felt herself dissolve, her body expanding into a burst of light. No book could have prepared her for this.

APPENDIX

Here are a few notes about the inspirations for these stories.

"Detective Mothman" – My non-cryptid books are mysteries, sometimes with a speculative or puzzle element. I'm a proud member of Sisters in Crime and a devotee of all things mystery. So I had to write a story about Mothman as a detective. There was one problem—Mothman is too frightening to do investigations himself. My kids and I used to read a picture book called *Shark Detective,* wherein the poor land-bound shark cannot function as a detective for the same reason. He pairs up with a cat who helps him charm the humans of Earth. I thought Mothman could do the same thing.

I also placed the story in Chicago because of the 2017 Mothman sightings there. There's an episode on the Netflix revival of *Unsolved Mysteries.* While I have been there many times, I have never lived in Chicago, so sending them around the city was a daunting task. I apologize for any errors. Nathan, Poppy, and Gene showed up in Andersonville because it is one of our favorite neighborhoods there.

"A Particular Melancholy" – When I mentioned to my friend Emily that I was writing a second cryptid book, she said, "You have to do the Squonk!" I had no idea what a Squonk was at the time, but after I looked it up, I knew I had to write the story. The Squonk is a Pennsylvanian creature found in the Poconos Mountains of northwestern Pennsylvania, about two hours from Philadelphia. There are many renderings of the Squonk online, but they all show it with folded skin and warts. I kept thinking of Clement from Buffy the Vampire Slayer, a wrinkly demon who eats kittens, although Phillip is too sweet to do that. Some legends say the Squonk is the one who cries, and people sucked in by its tears will be beholden to it forever or even die. Others say he feeds on sorrow, which is the concept I used to drive the story.

"Vanishing Twin Syndrome" – I was working in the teen room at my library one day and found a book full of monsters and legends, which is obviously my catnip. I took the book home and found a creature that intrigued me—the *strzyga*, a pair of twin demons that turn into vampires when they are separated. Specifically, one twin dies, and the other exacts revenge. I don't remember where I got the idea to turn them into a medical phenomenon, but since I love books and stories about medicine, it makes sense.

Strangely enough, one of my Duskbound colleagues, G.A. Finocchiaro, added similar creatures to his book *Suckers*; however, we each thought of the concept independently, and our versions are nothing alike. If you like dark paranormal comedy, give it a read.

"Guess Who's Coming to Dinner" – Another *Unsolved Mysteries* episode features the Bigfoot species that lives among the indigenous peoples of the American Southwest. This intrigued me, but I know nothing about the Southwest other than stopping in Albuquerque on a long-haul train trip (it was very hot and dry). I wondered what would happen if Southwest Bigfoot came home to Michigan Bigfoot. This story has a political message that doesn't make much sense at first. It didn't to me either; I had to figure out what I was saying after I said it.

Side note: thanks to my friend Kathryn for binge-watching the entire *Unsolved Mysteries* series and letting me know which ones I should watch.

"Wheel of Fortune" – This was the first story I wrote for this collection. I woke up one night freaking out after having a dream exactly like what happens to Maeve in her first nighttime horror. I had to figure out how to put it on the page. I generally do not borrow real humans for characters, but in this story I had to borrow my family so I could write the story the way I felt it in the dream. I then adjusted them in the edits so they weren't exact replicas. I did ask my kids what names they wanted. Henry didn't care, but Oliver requested the name of Bob. I went with Robert because that seemed like more of a little-kid name. He can decide if he wants to be a Bob when he gets older.

"My Stupid Time-Traveling Golem or Whatever" – My coworker, Michael Dober (who needs to be specified because I work with five Michaels), had been teasing me about the Peninsula Python. He was like, "That's not a cryptid, it's just a big snake." I can't remember how the discussion got turned this way, but he said something about turning a papier-mâché Bigfoot into a story. Thanks, Dober! It didn't work out in my mind as a Bigfoot, so a golem it was. The golem is a Hebrew legend and also appears in role-playing games such as Dungeons and Dragons and World of Warcraft, both of which I've sunk too much time into over the years.

"The Boy and the Crone" – I read the novel *Havoc* by Christopher Bollen and was fascinated by the idea of a boy and an old woman in a cat-and-mouse game. The author pulls it off way better than I do—I highly recommend this book. I tried to integrate it in a subtle way here as I twisted the story of Baba Yaga. She scares the crap out of me, but I thought that if I wormed my way into Crystal's head, the legend might be a little less scary. Because of the story's time period, Crystal is basically my age, and I tried to draw on her regrets and her disappointment that she never accomplished everything she wanted to. Marco has a lot of frustration because he wants to be a kid, but he's fenced in by so much, most specifically the environment and the insular nature of his community. He's a big personality who wants so much more.

"Even History Burns" – The aforementioned Peninsula Python was brought to my attention by my colleague Alex O'Sullivan (Alex is also a duplicated name at my work). I live ten minutes from Peninsula, so I had to write about it. Recently, the old Century Cycles building next to the railroad tracks burned down, as it happened in the story. I was really sad about this, so I thought I would bring that into the plot. As for the first-date story, I saw a couple people on a first date when my family was out at a pizza restaurant. I felt bad because they seemed so awkward, and I thought about how much pressure that might put on someone if they fundamentally disagreed. I could have been way more serious about that, but I thought Deb and Ross needed to have a little fun even if they weren't totally compatible.

"Grassman" – Another Cuyahoga Valley cryptid that I came across, the Grassman is like Northeast Ohio's version of Bigfoot, just a little smaller. Because Wendy and Deb had come across him in their younger years, I thought he deserved his own story, but I didn't have a spark for a full plot. My colleague Heidi thought it would be funny if he fell in love with a road cone. This is a little flash into his naïve, almost sweet mind. I wouldn't be surprised if I wrote a more detailed story about him once I have an idea that does his character justice.

"Save the Kids" – I've always admired the band The Civil Wars and wondered how they manage to get along while being divorced and singing together. I have never actually read about how that works out for them because I wanted to use that idea in a story. I'm sure they're fine and not nearly as volatile as Jack and Florence. I created them for "A Particular Melancholy" with the intention of developing their story separately alongside their kids' snooty private school. My original thought was to get more involved with the sneaky PTA and those women who all seem so cookie-cutter, but the story got a little off track from that. Which is just as well, because that stereotype has been done. I pulled closer into Florence's head than I originally intended, but I found there was a lot she needed to process.

"Bees and Lemons" – I listened to a lot of Tori Amos' *The Beekeeper* while writing this collection. It came out in 2004, but I've never forgotten the melancholy of the title track and "Toast," which explores her mother's illness and her brother's death, respectively. I did a cursory search for cryptids or myth that related to bees, but the magical element is 99% my own creation. I liked the idea that bees bring life and that lemons are yellow and sunny. I also had this image of death being a type of glittery explosion. If I go out that way, I'll be happy.

ACKNOWLEDGMENTS

I must start by thanking Kaytalin Platt McCarry, my friend and one of our Duskbound team members. I have no idea how many of my books Kaytalin has sold for me by designing such gorgeous covers. The whole "don't judge a book by its cover" thing is total bullshit. I've seen plenty of indie books that look like someone made the cover with Publisher and WordArt in 1995. Kaytalin's covers are eye-catching and professional, and my books feel "real" because of her. She gets me and my vision (so to speak, because that sounds like business nonsense). She also understands when I need to vent or when I'm feeling down about this writing stuff.

To all of my Duskbound colleagues—Mike X Welch, Aly Welch, G.A. Finocchiaro, and Kaytalin, of course—thank you so much for being you. I truly love reading all your work and being part of making your writing dreams successful too. I love that we can all discuss tough writing topics, collaborate on events, and brainstorm together.

Julie Hatcher, even by including you in every acknowledgments section, I can't thank you enough. You are a force of nature, endlessly working to provide for your kids and parents, selfless with love and vibrance. You deserve everything you've worked for and more.

L.A. McGinnis, I'm so glad I've gotten to know you more this year. I'm so grateful for your no-nonsense business sense and willingness to teach everyone in the Brain Trust about your ways. I'm in awe of your drive to put your books into your readers' hands.

To everyone else in my writers' groups and at work: I'm lucky to surround myself with all of you. Special props to all my coworkers who helped brainstorm (see the appendix if you haven't already). My coworkers are also hella talented, and if I do an illustrated version of this book, I'm sure you'll see more art from them. Check out the hardcover of I LOVED THE MOTHMAN if you haven't already.

Thank you to Celiah Aker and Alicia Frazier at Black Cat Books & Oddities for championing my books and recommending them to customers at your store. You've become such an asset to the city of Medina and the greater bookish community. You work so hard to bring delight to your patrons, and it shows.

To the Bassoon Bitches: Jen and Emily, you have been so supportive of this venture from the beginning, and I appreciate it so much! Thanks again to Emily for the Squonk idea and to both of you for inviting me to Akron Pops. The snark keeps me alive.

To my chosen family, Kathryn and Violet. Here's to more rides on Spaceship Earth and hopefully not in Portuguese.

Thanks to my therapist, Lorie, who is highly sane in the face of my neuroticism. Thanks to you, I've found some long-awaited healing, which gives me more space in my mind to daydream about creatures and myths.

Sorry to all the people I've forgotten to thank, or if I've thanked you in a previous book and not here. I'm still grateful!

Thanks to my sister, Jamie, for always being my biggest cheerleader.

Thank you to Ed, Henry, and Oliver for patiently dealing with me day after day.

www.ingramcontent.com/pod-product-compliance
Lightning Source LLC
Chambersburg PA
CBHW060450300726

48975CB00008B/2456